A Twelve Davis Christmas

****

Kitty Kaye

Cover Illustrated by
Debbe Femiak

To my Mom and Dad -
who taught us the
value of family,
and the importance
of spending time
together.

****

"A Twelve Davis Christmas is filled with laughter and tears, disappointment and triumph, and a testimony of the perseverance and love that embodies the heart of a parent. From the onset, author Kitty Kaye paints a fluid and fast-paced tale of the Davis family's unique celebration of Christmas replete with hilarious trials and joy-filled celebration that conjures all-too familiar memories unique to family life. Hold onto your seat, A Twelve Davis Christmas will leave you both refreshed and exhausted…in a good way!"

- Pastor David Grasso,
Life Fellowship Foursquare Church

****

The
Christmas
Plan

****

Chapter 1
The Christmas Plan

✯✯✯✯✯✯✯

It wasn't love at first sight. There were no magical sparks that lit the enchanted holiday air. It couldn't even have been considered a colorful event, other than the bright hue of red that slowly crept up Mary's neck, eventually capturing her entire face.

It could possibly have been described as a stand-off. Mary and Joseph stood across the festive holiday buffet table, fork in one hand and plate in the other, both laying claim to the same piece of meat on the tray filled with ham.

Looking at her eating utensil driven solidly into the rolled piece of meat, Mary noticed that another fork had joined hers. Attached to the fork was a very manly hand. Mary's gaze followed the hand up the tastefully decorated arm, then to the stately neck. The finely shaped chin above it was located just below the most gorgeous mouth she had ever seen. It was parted partially in a smile (was he laughing at her, or with her) and above that was a nose that was just as perfect as the rest of his face. But the eyes were like none she had ever seen before.

At first she thought she would never look away again, but then he spoke. She then realized that they seemed to be at odds, having a silent battle over an innocent piece of ham located centrally on the table between them.

"Did you want that piece of meat?" he asked, grinning playfully.

Her gaze returned quickly to the meat tray, which is what prompted the colors to begin to fly. As her face began to blossom with brilliant shades of red, she said, "Oh, I'm so sorry. I didn't mean to grab the same piece."

He said nothing, just stared at her with that exquisite

smile. She was almost mesmerized, and not sure she could speak intelligibly. However, she quickly found her tongue and said, "No, no - you can have the ham. I'll just grab a piece turkey."

Mary retrieved her fork from the piece of ham, and was aiming for the turkey, when he said, "No, no - you wanted the ham. Go ahead and take some. There's enough for both of us."

His charm and good looks made it hard for her to think straight. She smiled and said, "It doesn't really matter to me. I'm not hard to please. I would be happy with either ham or turkey."

"Would you just give her a piece of ham and get moving, Joseph?!" came a voice from somewhere behind them.

They had become so engulfed in one another that they had lost contact with their surroundings. Ben's comment brought them back to reality. Looking around, they realized there were people behind them who waiting for their turn to conquer the buffet table.

Joseph chuckled and asked Ben, "Do you think I should give her ham or turkey?"

Ben groaned and replied, "Just give her one piece of each and get on with it, man! I'm starving here! And the foods not getting any warmer."

Joseph plopped a piece of ham firmly on Mary's plate, followed by a piece of turkey.

"That should do it," he commented, smiling at her. "Sorry if I appeared greedy. I really wasn't trying to steal your food."

As he turned to walk away, Mary said, "That's quite all right. I wasn't trying to steal yours either."

Joseph returned to his table, located on the opposite side of the room. Mary tried to watch him go without being too obvious. She returned to her table with her co-workers from the business office. As she did, her mind was racing. She had worked for Newman Industries for three years now, and she had never crossed paths with Joseph before. How long had he been there? And why had she never seen him before?

"He's a charmer, isn't he?" Kayleigh commented. Kayleigh had worked with Mary in the business office for a couple of years, and they had become good friends.

"What?" Mary asked, absent-mindedly. She didn't realize she had been staring his way, but Kayleigh had noticed.

"Joseph," Kayleigh said. "You've been watching him ever since you came back from the buffet table. Did you just notice him?"

"Kind of," Mary said, blushing a bit as she remembered their encounter at the food table. "Do you know him?"

"His name is Joseph Davis," Kayleigh explained. "He works in shipping and receiving."

"How long has he been at Newman?" Mary pursued.

"For over a year now, I would guess," Kayleigh answered.

He had worked for Newman Industries for over a year and Mary had never noticed him before? How could that be? Perhaps their paths had never crossed before, but Mary would be sure they crossed again.

****

Mary didn't see Joseph again for several weeks. She looked for opportunities, excuses, and even silly reasons to go to Shipping on errands. Yet, she never seemed to spot Joseph. Had he just been an illusion, a figment of her imagination? She didn't think her imagination could be that creative, or capable of developing such a fine human specimen. He had to be real.

Then one day, when she least expected it, there he was again. She was just coming out of the cafeteria and almost ran straight into him.

"Joseph - hi," Mary said shyly.

"So you know my name," he smiled. He waited for her to introduce herself, but she just stood there and smiled shyly.

10

So he asked, "And you would be?"

"Oh, I'm sorry," she apologized. "My name is Mary. We met at the holiday party."

"Yes, I remember," Joseph smiled. "You like ham….. and turkey, too!"

Mary chuckled and said, "Yes, it's true. I hadn't seen you since then, so I was beginning to think I had imagined our first encounter."

"Not true," Joseph said. "It really happened."

They stood looking at each other awkwardly for a moment. Then Joseph took a chance and asked, "Are you interested in another encounter? I'm free tomorrow night."

"Oh," Mary said, taken by surprise. She knew she couldn't let him disappear again, so she quickly seized the opportunity and replied that she was indeed free.

"What time do you get out of work? Maybe we could go grab some pizza," Joseph said.

"That sounds great," Mary agreed. "I'm off at 5:00. Do you want to meet me at the office?"

"Sounds like a date," Joseph said. "We'll just get plain pizza, and then we won't have to fight over ham or turkey!"

****

That was the beginning of their whirlwind romance. It may not have been love at first sight, but it was definitely love at second, third and fourth sight. And fifth, and sixth, and seventh……

Mary had never felt so alive and happy in her entire life. And as for Joseph, it was pretty much the same. They approached each day with a new excitement. It wasn't the usual dread of having to go to work. They would race to work each morning, where they would meet in the cafeteria for a cup of coffee. Each break found them there again, and lunch time was pure bliss. A full half hour to stare into each others eyes, and share ham and turkey sandwiches!

With names like Mary and Joseph, it must have been a match made in Heaven. And having met at the holiday party, they knew that Christmas was always going to be a special time for them. So the following year on Christmas Eve, Mary Martell relinquished her maiden name and took on the title of Mrs. Mary Davis, wife of Joseph Davis.

****

It was a blissful first year of love and romance. Each day they felt a little more blessed than the day before. Mary conceived quickly, and the following Christmas, they gave birth to their firstborn son. And no, even though their names were Mary and Joseph, they did not wrap him in swaddling clothes and lay him in a manger. And they did not name him Jesus. They named him Luke, after their favorite version of the Christmas story.

They proved to be a fertile couple, bearing fruit almost annually. Luke was soon followed by brothers, Beau and Joseph Jr. Mary and Joseph decided to pursue holiday names and blessed the remaining children with names like Noel, Gloria, Garland (whom they nicknamed Gary,) Candy, Nicholas, Angel, Berry, Star, and Joy. A full dozen in just a couple of decades.

With so many children and schedules to keep track of, Mary found it too difficult to work. She soon became a stay-at-home mom, and Joseph worked extra hours to make ends meet. There were times when Mary thought she would not survive the demands placed on her by her offspring, but Joseph proved to be a devoted husband and father. He was always available for moral support for Mary, and provided the necessary discipline and advice for his tribe of children.

Although, at times it seemed to take light years to raise the brood, the youngest child finally moved out and Mary and Joseph could breathe again. It's not that they didn't love their children. Each child had a very special place in their hearts, but finally they could stop chasing children and take some time to rest. And without so many kids to cart along, they were finally able to travel. The highlight of their retirement from the child-bearing years was a foreign trip to Europe -visiting Germany, Austria and France.

For several years after the children moved out, they attempted to have a family gathering at Christmastime. But the family proved to be too big for such an endeavor. Not only were there the original twelve siblings, but the family now included spouses, boyfriends, and girlfriends. And when the grandchildren started to come along, it became obvious that their big, old Colonial house just wasn't large enough to accommodate the needs of their family gatherings.

Mary and Joseph realized something had to be done. Christmas just wasn't a celebration anymore. There were too many sibling squabbles, and the bickering over the bathroom was out of control. Renting the local town hall didn't work well either. Mary and Joseph were so exhausted with the events of each Christmas Day, they couldn't seem to enjoy the holiday. Christmas had lost its magic and splendor.

So they devised a creative family holiday plan, one which they hoped to employ on an annual basis. They would schedule one day for each child to come visit. That way, there would be no chaos or confusion. No carting everything to a foreign banquet hall to meet. No jealousy about who got what. No siblings comparing notes about whose child was brighter, or smarter, or better dressed. Only individually focused attention from mom and dad on one offspring and their family at a time.

Of course, it was Mary's idea.

"You remember the song about the Twelve Days of Christmas?" she asked Joseph one day.

"Yes, of course," Joseph replied, wondering what Mary was up to this time.

"Well, why don't we just have a Twelve Davis Christmas?!" she asked excitedly. "We will have one Davis child come home each day for twelve days of Christmas celebration."

"No wonder I married you," Joseph had replied. "You are one clever lady. I think that just might work."

And so began the annual tradition of the Twelve Davis Christmas. Each child would be invited home for their own one-on-one Christmas encounter with mom and dad.

"This will be so wonderful," Mary and Joseph agreed. "No challenge, no mega family drama. Just one day at a time, and it will stretch Christmas out for a full twelve days. Next year the holidays are going to be simply awesome."

And with Joseph in full agreement, Mary began her plans for the Christmas celebrations – celebrating the holiday cheer with one child at a time for twelve fun-filled days of Christmas.

****

Luke

****

Chapter 2
Luke

✱✱✱✱✱✱✱

It was Day One of the first Davis twelve days of Christmas plan. Mary Davis awoke with a spirit of excitement brewing inside. It was still an early hour of the morning, but she soon realized her efforts to return to sleep were futile. She was simply too excited about the next twelve days to go back to sleep. So she decided to head downstairs to do some baking.

She left Joseph snoring in bed and wandered down to the kitchen to brew a cup of coffee. Yesterday, she had made lasagna and a chocolate cream pie for dinner today, but the homemade rolls that Luke loved so much still needed to be made. They were best when piping hot, so she had decided to wait until today to make them. And if she had time, she might make a batch of chocolate chip cookies for Luke to take home. Being a bachelor, she knew he would appreciate some good old-fashioned home-baked goods.

Mary had put a lot of thought and planning into this twelve day schedule. She had designed a scene for the front door for each of her children. She excitedly thought about how this was going to be the best twelve days of the year, and wondered why she hadn't thought of it sooner.

She pulled the necessary ingredients from the kitchen cupboards and, after gulping a few swallows of coffee, began the baking process. As she worked, she pondered the significance of the name they had given their firstborn son. They had chosen the name as it was their favorite Biblical version of the Christmas story.

It had always amazed Mary that in telling the world of the birth of His son, God had chosen to announce it to a group of lowly shepherds, huddling around a campfire in a dark field with a bunch of sleeping sheep. If it had been up to her, she would have marched right into the throne room of the king and announced that his replacement had arrived.

Mary smiled as she pictured herself boldly tramping into a royal throne room. But her smile quickly faded when she envisioned the king's expression at her announcement. His position was one of authority, and he might not appreciate her barging into his throne room to tell him he was going to be replaced. Plus, he held the power of life and death in his hand.

As if a light went on in her head, Mary suddenly understood why God had chosen to share His news with shepherds. They would embrace the glad tidings with great joy a whole lot more than a king who felt threatened.

I guess God did know what He was doing, Mary smiled to herself. *But then, He usually does*!

So deep in thought was Mary, that she failed to hear her sleepy husband approaching the kitchen. Looking up to find someone standing there startled Mary beyond reason. She reacted impulsively, doing the first thing that came to mind. Before she realized what she was doing, the cup of flour she held in her hand flew across the room and struck her husband in the head.

Joseph couldn't believe that his wife had just greeted him with a fresh coating of flour. His forehead stung where the cup had struck him, and his glasses were completely covered so he couldn't see her expression. For a moment, he stood in stunned silence. Then he cleared his throat and addressed his wife.

"Mary, why did you just throw flour in my face?" he questioned.

"I didn't know you were here," she replied, grabbing a dish towel and furtively trying to brush the flour off her husband.

Joseph blew the flour from his lips and stated, "I have been here for about forty years now."

"I know that, Joseph!" Mary said, exasperated. "It's just that I didn't hear you coming. I was deep in thought and was under the impression that you were still in bed."

"I wish I was," Joseph said dryly. "At least when I was in bed, I wasn't covered with flour."

"Oh, Joseph," said Mary, rustling his hair to try to brush the flour out. "I'm sorry. And it could have been worse. I could have thrown the whole bowl at you. That would have woken you up quickly, a metal bowl bouncing off your head."

"Such a practical lady," Joseph muttered, more to himself than to Mary. "I think I will go take a shower now, and try starting this day over again."

"Good idea," Mary agreed. "I'll clean this mess up and finish baking before Luke gets here."

Joseph turned to walk away and looked back over his shoulder as if he were expecting another flying object to hit his retreating back.

Seeing him watching her, Mary said softly, "I'm sorry! I really am!"

Joseph smiled and walked away. Such a wonderful, exasperating women – but amazing just the same.

****

Mary could hardly wait for Luke to arrive and the Christmas celebrations to begin. For Luke's day, she had decorated the front door with a picture of a shepherd boy, adorned with a decorative name tag. And of course, she had added a fluffy, little lamb.

Joseph had rejoined her following his shower. She had found a few clumps of pasty flour in his hair, but felt she had successfully removed most of them. Now they awaited Luke's arrival.

Although Luke was the oldest, he had never married. He had become an advertising executive, who had invested his time and passion into vintage autos, starting his own vintage auto shop as a secondary career. And so Mom and Dad were not surprised when Luke roared into the driveway a short time later in an absolutely picture perfect 1964 Ford Mustang. Every inch of it looked like it had just been polished, including the chrome.

Mary quickly headed for the door, but Joseph stopped her.

"Just relax, Mom," he chided her. "Let the boy come through the door on his own. He's a big boy, you know."

"I know," Mary replied, "but it always seems like it's been forever since I've seen him."

"You sound like it's been years," Dad teased.

Luke approached the front door, and seeing it decorated with a shepherd and his little lamb, he chuckled to himself.

"Cute, Mom," he mumbled, "real cute!"

Mary could restrain herself no longer. She threw open the front door and excitedly yelled, "Luke" while dragging him into her arms.

"Geesh, Mom," Luke said. "You act like you haven't seen me for years!"

"I'm just so excited about Christmas this year," Mary explained. "It will be so nice having just one child at a time. We can still have our annual picnic in the summertime, where the kids can run and play and enjoy time together - outside! But at Christmastime, it's gonna be just one sibling at a time with Mom and Dad's undivided attention."

Luke chuckled at his mother's excitement and asked, "So, what types of activities do you have planned?"

Mary's eyes lit up as she described items on the agenda for the next twelve days.

"Well, we are helping Joy with the tree lighting this year," looking adoringly at her husband, she added, "and your father will be playing the esteemed role of Santa Claus."

"How did you get roped into that one, Dad?" Luke asked.

Before he could reply, Mary jumped in and said, "Because he heard Margaret Wellington was going to be Mrs. Claus!"

Joseph rolled his eyes, shook his head and said,

"Hardly, Mary. That would be my reason for not wanting to be Santa." Looking at his son, he added, "Joy said she needed help, so I volunteered. Your mother isn't too happy that her arch enemy will be playing Mrs. Claus, but it's just for one night. And if it doesn't go well, next year Margaret Wellington will just have to find herself a new man!"

Everyone chuckled, then Mary continued with the plans. "We plan on sledding with Gary and the kids at the local park, we are going to see one of Angel's twins in the live nativity, and Berry wants us to go skiing with him at Dorr Mountain on his day."

She looked hesitantly at both men, almost with a shade of panic showing.

"You might notice your mother is a bit concerned about that day," Joseph said to Luke.

"It's been a long time since you've been on skiis, Mom," Luke commented.

"Don't I know it," she replied. "But we will give it a try. And, hopefully, we will live through it...."

"Berry and Olivia will be there to help you," Luke reassured them. "So what about the other days?"

"Nothing set in stone yet. I'm sure Morgan will want to go to the mall on Nick's day," Mary added, "but the rest of the time we will just go with the flow."

"Like you always have, right, Mom?" Luke smiled at his mom. "Well, I hope all goes as well as the two of you are hoping."

Mary grabbed Luke's hand and pulled him into the living room. "Oh, Luke," she scolded, "what could possibly go wrong?"

"I want to say nothing," Luke stated, "but....you did raise twelve kids, and you know things don't always turn out as planned....."

Mary gave her oldest son a brief look of concern, knowing that he did have a good point. She had found quite frequently during the busy years of parenting, that it was always good to have a backup plan.

Seeing his mother's look of concern, Luke quickly changed the subject and said, "I have to run outside for a minute. I left my girlfriend in the car."

"You have a girlfriend!" Mary said with excitement.

Luke gave his mother a mischievous smile, and then headed out the door. Mom didn't know what to think. Luke had never mentioned a girlfriend to her before, and it didn't seem right that he had made her sit in the car all this time instead of bringing her in with him. She tried to busy herself straightening the couch cushions while she waited for his return.

His return came in a bit of a flurry. Luke came running through the front door, sheltering something in his arms, with a chorus of barking behind him. He quickly slammed the door and turned to lean on it.

"Whose dog is that?!" Luke asked, a bit winded.

Dad looked out the window at Buzzy, still barking ferociously at the closed front door.

"Oh, that's just Buzzy," he explained. "He's kind of the neighborhood dog. He doesn't really belong to anyone. He sort of belongs to all of us. He just buzzes around from house to house. That's how he got his name."

"Well, I guess he doesn't like me," Luke said.

"At least you don't have a uniform on. He really hates uniforms and costumes," Dad explained. "On Halloween, someone has to lock him in their garage, because he just can't handle all the costumes."

Mom looked at the furry little bundle in Luke's arms and said, "And its not you anyway, Luke. It's that cute little bundle you are holding."

Luke looked down at the kitten in his arms like he had forgotten he was holding it. He looked up at his mother and smiled. "Mom, I would like you to meet my new girlfriend," he said proudly. "When I saw this little cutie, I thought she would make a perfect companion. And now you can't say I live alone."

Mom smiled as she reached out and took the kitten

from Luke. "She is adorable. What did you name her?"

"I sort of named her after you," Luke replied. "I kept the Christmas theme and named her Merry. It sounds the same, but it's spelled like Merry Christmas. It suits her well, because she is a merry little thing."

Now that Luke had made it safely into the house with the kitten, and had proudly shown off his girlfriend, he took a moment to look around. Spotting the Christmas tree, he was surprised to see that it was undecorated.

"No decorations on the tree this year, Mom?" he asked.

"Oh, I couldn't decorate it without the children," she explained. "We decided to put it up, but wait for the grandchildren to arrive to help with the decorations. It just isn't the same decorating it alone. You need to be able to share the memories and stories behind each ornament with someone, and why not do that with the next generation."

"Sounds like a good plan, Mom," Luke said. "You are always thinking ahead."

"That's just who I am, Luke," Mom smiled. "Always making plans…."

Luke smiled, gave his mother a quick hug, and then turned his attention to his father.

"So, what have you been up to in your retirement, Dad? Are you keeping busy?"

Dad chuckled and said, "Have I ever. Let me show you some of the projects I've been working on."

Dad led Luke into the den where the shelves were lined with books. "You know how I have collected my favorite books throughout the years. Sometimes I think I have more books than the library!"

Luke looked around and chuckled. The collection may not have been as large as the library's, but it was definitely a good start.

"Yeah, a good portion of the collection was gifts from your children, I'm sure," said Luke. "At least you made it easy for us to buy birthday gifts and Christmas presents for you!"

"Yes, you kids definitely helped add to the collection.

Well, now that I have more free time on my hands, I have been able to organize them all by author. Now I can find the book I want without having to go through them all."

"Nice, Dad," said Luke, tipping his head sideways to look at some of the titles. "You've got quite a system here. Very organized, indeed."

Luke's gaze scanned the rest of the room and came to rest on the cuckoo clock mounted on the wall.

"And I see you have Mom's cuckoo clock from Germany in its place finally," he said.

"Oh, yes. Mom didn't stop nagging me until I got that hung," he chuckled. "It was a challenge to find the perfect spot, though."

Mom came in just then, still cuddling the kitten from Luke, and said, "Well, Joseph, I didn't cart that clock all the way back from Germany just to leave it in the box. I wanted it hanging on the wall where everyone can see and enjoy it as much as I have."

"So how was your trip to Europe?" Luke questioned.

Mom smiled and said, "Nothing short of spectacular!" Pointing to the end tables beside the couch, Mom added, "And come look at this Tiffany lamp from Paris and the vase we brought back from Vienna."

Luke walked over to check out the Tiffany lamp, and shot his mother a sideward glance.

"You brought a Tiffany lamp all the way back from Europe?" he asked.

His mother gave an eager nod.

He smiled and said, "You could have just gone to New York to buy one, you know. They do make them in America."

Mary returned his smile and replied, "I know, but I fell in love with this one in Paris, and just had to have it. Having raised twelve children, I have not had the good fortune of spoiling myself through the years."

Joseph joined the conversation and added, "Plus I insisted. Your mother was so excited when she found it, and I thought she deserved something special."

Mary gave her husband a loving smile, and he winked playfully back at her. The silent interaction caught Luke's watchful eye, and he couldn't help but grin. Over forty years and twelve kids later, and his parents were still in love.

Turning his attention back to the fragile souvenirs, Luke raised his eyebrows and said, "The amazing thing is that you managed to get it all home safely. That was a feat in itself!"

Luke advanced to the end tables to get a closer look at the souvenirs.

Dad, chuckling at Luke's comment, said, "You know when we were flying out, we saw the way they handled the suitcases at the airport. So we shipped them home rather than trying to carry them back in our suitcases."

"Probably a good idea," Luke agreed. "The last time I flew, the officials couldn't get my suitcase unlocked, so they cut the tabs off the zipper. It was pretty close to useless by the time they were done with it. Why didn't they just cut the lock off instead of ruining the suitcase?!"

Luke looked around the room and said, "So, show me what else you've been up to in your spare time, Dad."

"Well, step this way, son," Dad said, leading the trio into the kitchen. "Mom was complaining that she didn't have enough counter space, so I built this island for her."

Luke was clearly impressed with his father's craftsmanship. "You made this?!" he asked, incredulously. When Dad nodded his head in affirmation, Luke added, "I am truly impressed! I didn't know you were so talented!"

Dad chuckled and said, "I don't know if I'm improving with age, or if it's just that I have more time to work on things now. But I thought it came out pretty decent."

"And look at this," Mom said, pointing to the spice rack sitting on the kitchen counter. "I have always had a hard time organizing my spices, so Dad made me a spice rack. Now I can find what I want. All my baking spices are on one shelf and all my cooking spices are on the other. No more digging around in the cupboard and emptying it out every time I can't find the spice I want."

"Oh, yeah," said Dad, "and look out the window."

Luke moved over to join Dad in front of the window located over the kitchen sink. Dad continued, "See the recycling center I built? Now we can organize our cans, bottles, and waste paper for recycling."

Luke was just short of amazed with his father's abilities. "Dad! You are getting so organized in your old age!"

Dad let out a rolling rumble of laughter. "Oh, yes, and just in time for senile dementia to set in. But, hopefully, we will be so organized that you kids will be able to figure out where we left everything!"

"Oh, Joseph," Mary said, "you have a few more years before you need to worry about that!"

"At least he will be a good-looking, senile old man," Luke laughed.

Mary looked up at her oldest son with love in her eyes. "Yes, your Dad has definitely retained his good looks, even though he is pretty gray now."

"Enough so that Margaret Wellington is still hot on his tail?" Luke questioned.

Mom shot her son a cautionary look, and Dad stepped in to the rescue. "Better not bring that name up often," he warned his son, jokingly. "Mom is not any too fond of that lady."

"Why should I be?" Mom questioned. "She openly flirts with my husband, right in front of me. 'Oh, Joey, you are looking simply wonderful today.'" Mary imitated Margaret. "Who calls him Joey, anyway?!"

Simultaneously, Joseph and Luke replied, "She does!!!"

Mary just shook her head. "That woman is such a nag. No wonder her husband died at an early age. She probably nagged him to death."

Both men chuckled and shook their heads. "You might be right, Mom," Luke agreed with his mother, and Joseph simply nodded in reply.

Having shown Luke all the new features that had been added since his last visit, Dad turned his attention to his eldest son.

"So, what have you been up to, Luke?" he asked.

Luke just shrugged and said, "Oh, the usual. Working every day at the office and keeping my shop going on the side. Gotta keep the shelves stocked for all the auto buffs like me, still trying to make that vintage car perfect."

"And no new girlfriends or companions?" Mom asked hopefully, then added, "Other than Merry, I mean?!"

Luke tipped his head and looked at his mother sideways. "Mom, you know me. I'm busy with my cars. And, if there was a new girlfriend, you would probably be the first to know."

"I know, I know," said Mom, "but I just keep hoping. I just want you to be happy, and it seems to me that you would be happier if you had someone to share your life with."

"I am happy, Mom," Luke insisted. "Being the oldest of twelve, I enjoy having a nice quiet house to go home to at night. If I get lonely, I have Merry to talk to and snuggle up with. And I do date, you know, just nothing serious."

Dad put his arm around his wife's shoulder and said, "You know your mother. She loved having a houseful of people, so it's hard for her to understand how anyone could be happy living alone. But if you're happy, then we are, too."

Quickly changing the subject so as not to upset their time together, Dad asked, "So what car have you been working on lately?"

Luke's face brightened. "I have just finished fixing up my dream car - a '64 Mustang. I brought it with me. Do you want to take a look?"

"Oh, yes! We would love to see it," chorused Mom and Dad. Mary picked up her namesake and the group headed outside to check out the car parked in the yard.

Walking across the front yard, Mom and Dad could already see that Luke had done an excellent job. The car was immaculate. Luke had spared nothing to make sure it was restored to perfection.

"Nice paint job," Dad commented.

"Oh, Luke," sighed Mom, "she's a beauty!"

"Thanks," Luke grinned. "This is the car I have always wanted. I just happened to come across it. One of my customers wanted to get rid of it. It needed a lot of work, but I knew it would be gorgeous when I was done with it."

"And so she is indeed," agreed Dad.

While inspecting the car, Sam the neighborhood mailman walked by. Attached to his pant leg, and growling as usual, was Buzzy. The Davis group momentarily stopped their perusing of Luke's car to watch the sight. Sam walked along as if it was nothing unusual to have a dog attached to his leg.

He glanced up from the letters he had been browsing through, and saw the three pair of eyes focused on him. Smiling cheerfully, he said, "Good afternoon, Joseph.....Mary. Is that Luke I see?"

Surprised that Sam was still delivering mail in the neighborhood, and even more surprised that he remembered his name, Luke said, "And so it is. Good to see you, Sam. How have you been?"

But before Sam could reply, Buzzy took over center stage. The conversation had caught his attention, and what Mary held in her arms was much more interesting than Sam's cotton pant leg. He could chew on that any time, but a cute, little kitten was not easy to come by. Narrowing his focus in on Merry, he let loose of Sam's pants like they were covered with jalapeno hot sauce and shot straight across the Davis yard. He cared not that he was outnumbered four human adults to one little bulldog. All he saw was a furry, little bundle that needed to know he was in charge.

Before anyone knew what was happening, Merry had jumped from Mom's arms to the top of Luke's Mustang. And Buzzy was not stopping, just because there was a car in his way. Having gained momentum as he ran across the yard, he took a flying leap to try to reach the kitten on the top of the car. He failed to reach her, but his claws sunk deep into the fresh paint job, and he dragged them the full length of the door. But he didn't stop there. He continued to jump on the car, leaving more and more scratch marks on the door.

"No, Buzzy!" screamed Mom.

"Stop, Buzzy!" demanded Dad.

"My car!" yelled Luke.

Sam, the mailman, just stood quietly watching in disbelief. Having dragged Buzzy around the neighborhood for years, he knew he was quite capable of anything. But he had never seen him cause destruction like this. Luke's beautiful car was now covered with "Buzzy" track marks down the full length of the passenger door. He briefly contemplated how he could help, but Mary was quick to jump into action. She grabbed Merry from the top of the car and ran back into the house. Joseph grabbed Buzzy by the collar and dragged him to the end of the driveway.

Once the kitten was gone, Buzzy's challenge was, too. At first he appeared to sulk, like a freshly scolded child. But looking up, he saw Sam was still there, so he quickly resumed his position of tugging on his pant leg.

Sam glanced down at the ferocious dog once again pulling on his pants, then looked up at the Davis men and shook his head.

"I have hoped for years that some day he would either have a heart attack or run away," he called over to them. "But it looks like I'm just destined to be stuck with him."

With that, he waved a farewell and continued his trek down the sidewalk. Looking back over his shoulder, he added, "Sorry about your car, Luke."

"Thanks, Sam," Luke called back, appreciating Sam's sympathy.

Sam went back to sorting through the mail in his hands, and dragging the deranged dog along with him, as if it was natural and meant to be.

Joseph shook his head and chuckled. Looking at his eldest son, he said, "That poor man will probably walk with a limp when he retires, having dragged that dog around for so many years."

"He's got more patience than I have," Luke replied.

"Me, too," Joseph agreed. "If he grabbed my pant leg, I would probably whack him over the head!"

Mary returned from depositing the kitten in the house, and the three of them turned their attention to Luke's car to inspect the damage that had been done.

"I'm so sorry, Luke," Mom said.

"That dog can be so unpredictable," Dad explained. "I'm so sorry about the damage done to your car."

Luke stood, shook his head, and tried to maintain an upbeat attitude. "Guess I'll just have to paint it again," he said. Then looking at Mom he added, "Now you know why I don't have any girlfriends. My cars take up all my time and money!"

"Oh, Luke," Mom said, smacking him playfully. "It's just an excuse! Just another one of your silly excuses!"

"Fortunately, I have some paint left over," Luke said, still thoughtfully considering the damage done to his car door. "So the color will match, and it should be a quick fix."

Joseph smiled at his son and said, "I guess we know what you acquired from your mother – her positive attitude!"

He turned to smile at his wife, and she gave him an appreciative smile in return. Luke smiled and gave his mother a hug. He didn't mind having inherited her attitude. She was the most positive person he knew.

"Come on in and have some lunch," Mary told her men. Looking at Luke, she added, "I made your favorite food."

"Lasagna?!" Luke asked, hopefully.

"With homemade rolls and chocolate cream pie for dessert," Mary triumphantly announced.

Luke smiled and gave his mother a huge hug. "You're the best, Mom!"

"That she is," Joseph agreed, as the threesome turned to make their way back into the house.

Together, the trio dined and laughed together over Luke's special meal. Having had twelve kids in the family with lots of childhood antics per child, there was a lot to reminisce about. As they chatted and laughed, Mary came to a conclusion.

"You know, the funniest memories seem to be the ones that upset me the most at the time they occurred," she commented.

Luke smiled and said, "Like the time we were throwing the pillow around the living room while we were watching TV?"

They all laughed, remembering the outcome of the situation.

"Your mother wasn't laughing that day," Joseph commented.

Mary said, "Well, wearing my cup of ice tea because Joey had poor timing when he threw the pillow wasn't really too funny at the time."

They all paused to picture the mother of the tribe standing in frustration, holding an empty glass in her hand while the drops of iced tea that her clothes had not absorbed ran through her hair and down her face.

Mary chuckled again, and added, "Not funny then, but definitely worth a laugh now!"

After dinner was done, Dad and Luke sat down to watch a game together while Mom cleaned the kitchen.

When the afternoon had faded, Luke picked up Merry and announced it was time for him to head home. His parents accompanied him to his car, thanked him for coming, and reflected on what a fun day it had been. Upon arriving at the car, Luke quickly tucked Merry inside, just incase Buzzy should reappear.

Then turning to his parents, he asked, "Is Beau coming tomorrow?"

"That's the plan," Joseph responded.

"I hope he doesn't have any trouble," Mary added. "It's supposed to snow during the night."

"Oh, you know Beau," Luke chuckled. "He doesn't usually have trouble getting to places he wants to be." He smiled and gave his mother one last hug. "Plus, he lives just around the corner, Mom!"

Mother, father and son had one last round of hugs, with Mary and Joseph once more apologizing profusely for the damage Buzzy had caused to the newly restored car. Luke again reassured him it wasn't anything he couldn't fix.

Mary ran back inside to retrieve the chocolate chip cookies she had made for Luke to take home, and they sent him on his way. After waving good-bye, Joseph turned his attention to Mary.

"That worked very well, my dear," Joseph complimented his wife. "I think your plan of having one child come each day was a clever one."

Mary, having had the brunt of raising the brood, wasn't so convinced. "I guess time will tell, Joseph," she said. "This may have just been the calm before the storm..."

"Oh, don't go negative on me, Mary," Joseph chided his wife. "Like Luke surmised, you have been planning this for a whole year now, and I'm sure you have each day completely mapped out. We both know what a good planner you are. So we will just take it one day at a time and remain positive and focused."

"Sounds like a plan to me," Mary agreed with her husband. Then wrapping their arms around each other, they turned and walked back to their empty, quiet, peaceful house.

****

✶✶✶✶✶✶✶

Beau

✶✶✶✶✶✶✶

Chapter 3
Beau

☆☆☆☆☆☆☆

Beau arrived on Day Two amidst the new fallen snow, accompanied by his eleven-year old son, Oliver. He had been a single dad since Oliver's mother had left, just shy of six years ago. She still called occasionally, and always sent cards for his birthday, but raising Oliver had been primarily Beau's responsibility. It had proven to be more of a challenge then Beau had expected.

It's not that Oliver was a mischievous or poorly behaved child, but more that he was a klutzy, awkward one. If there was an accident to be had, Oliver would have it. Trouble just seemed to follow him everywhere he went.

Oliver was excited to visit Grandma and Grandpa Davis. When Beau pulled into the yard, Oliver quickly jumped out of the car and ran for the house. As he arrived at the front door, he stopped to admire the "Beau" sign Grandma Mary had made and decorated with a giant Christmas bow.

"Look, Dad," he called back to his father, who was just coming up the walkway behind him. "Grandma made a sign for you!"

Beau smiled and said, "So she did!"

The always inquisitive Oliver reached up to touch the bow. But as he did, the sleeve of his jacket got caught on it and almost tore the sign in two.

"Uh-oh," he said, looking at his father with a horrified expression.

Beau just patted him on the head and said, "Don't worry about it, son. I'm sure Grammy plans to throw the sign out anyway."

Just then the front door flew open, and Mary and Joseph boisterously greeted the newcomers. Hugs and kisses abounded, and then Grandma paused to take a look at Oliver.

"Why, Oliver - I think you grow at least two inches between every visit," she said, wrapping her arms around him again.

"Good to see you, Beau," said Joseph, shaking his hand and patting him on the back.

Mary and Joseph ushered their guests inside, and Grandma Mary quickly started announcing plans for the day.

"So, as you can see, Oliver," she said, pointing to her undecorated tree, "my Christmas tree needs some help. I thought maybe you could be my official tree decorating assistant."

"Sure," beamed Oliver, "I love to decorate Christmas trees."

"You need to be very careful with the ornaments," warned Beau. "You're kind of like a bull in a china shop."

Looking at his mother and father, Beau added, "If it's breakable, Oliver will be the one to break it."

"Beau, don't talk like that," scolded Mary.

"You weren't so graceful yourself, son," Joseph reminded him.

"But I wasn't as much of a clutz as my son, Oliver," Beau insisted.

"You just need to give him time," Mary said, giving Oliver a reassuring hug. "He's just a growing boy. His body will catch up with him eventually."

"Okay, if you say so," Beau grinned.

"Beau, why don't you and I have a cup of coffee while Oliver helps Grandma decorate the tree," suggested Joseph.

Grandma Mary opened her box of Christmas decorations and went to work unwrapping keepsake ornaments. As she did, she explained the story behind each one to Oliver. All seemed to be going quite well, with both individulas deeply involved in the project. Finally Grandma Mary came to her favorite ornament of all, buried deep in the bottom of the box for safe-keeping.

"Oh, look at this one, Oliver," Grandma Mary gasped. "This one is my favorite. It's a hand-blown glass ornament that Grandpa Joseph bought for me when we visited Bermuda."

"It's beautiful, Grammy," admired Oliver.

"We always put this one near the top of the tree so it doesn't get bumped or knocked off," Grandma Mary explained. "Would you like the honor of hanging it?"

"Really?" asked Oliver. "You would let me do that?!"

He was awed that Grandma Mary would give him such an honor, especially after his dad had warned her of his mishaps.

"Why, of course I'll let you hang it," Grandma Mary smiled. "You'll have to stand on a chair to reach that high, though."

She pulled a chair over and Oliver gingerly climbed onto the seat. He delicately took the ornament from his grandmother and cautiously turned to hang it on the tree. However, just as he thought he had successfully accomplished the task, he lost his balance and toppled out of the chair. Unfortunately, the ornament had not reached its intended target on the tree and followed Oliver on his route to the floor. And not only did Grandma Mary's favorite ornament meet its fate as it crashed onto the floor, but a few others joined it on the way.

Hearing the crash, Beau and his father came rushing into the living room. Oliver was just rising from his landing zone on the floor, which was surrounded by scattered pieces of broken glass from the ornaments. It was obvious that he was close to tears, but before Beau could scold him, Mary spoke up.

"Oh, Oliver, don't worry about it," she comforted him. "It was an accident. You lost your balance. Those things happen sometimes."

Grandpa Joseph was determined to save the situation and help rebuild Oliver's self-confidence. Thinking quickly, he came up with a new task for him.

"Why don't you take my new shovel outside and do some work for me. You can shovel a path from the back door to my new recycling center. Your grandmother and I will clean this up," he suggested.

Oliver was quick to comply with his grandfather's request. He would show them that he could do something constructive. He would shovel a path for them in no time, probably before they could finish cleaning up the last mess he had made.

The adults set to work sweeping and cleaning up the broken ornaments while Oliver went outside to shovel the snow.

"Oh, Mom, I am so sorry about your ornaments," Beau began. "I know how special they are to you, each one with a tale to tell. But I warned you that he is an awkward boy."

Mary held the dust pan while Joseph swept the broken pieces into it. "Oh, Beau, he just lost his balance," she said, defending her grandson.

"So true," agreed Beau, "but that's the problem. He's always losing his balance, or breaking this, or breaking that. He's eleven years old, and I still have to kid-proof my house and buy everything in plastic. I've never seen a kid like him before."

"He'll improve in time," insisted Joseph.

"I sure hope so," Beau said, "and I hope I still have a house left by then!"

Grandma Mary swept up the last piece of broken glass and said, "There, that takes care of that. Everything is back to normal now."

"Except the missing ornaments," said Beau sadly. Brightening up, he said, "But it will give you and dad a reason to go back to Bermuda again."

Mary and Joseph chuckled. "I don't think we will go all the way back to Bermuda just to buy a new Christmas ornament," Joseph said.

"But we could....." Mary said dreamily.

Just then a little voice from the back of the room timidly called, "Grandpa?"

Oliver stepped into the room, holding something behind

his back.

"What's up, Oliver?" Grandpa Joseph questioned.

Oliver pulled the shovel out from behind him to reveal a broken handle. "I broke your shovel," he explained, once again looking sad and close to tears.

Joseph exchanged glances with Beau. Maybe he was right. Oliver did seem to be accident prone. But Grandpa Joseph remained upbeat. This was Beau and Oliver's special day, and he wasn't going to let a few broken ornaments, or a severed shovel handle, spoil the day.

"You know, Oliver, I have a project I need some help with," Grandpa Joseph said. "Do you think you could help me hang some lights on the outside of the house?"

Oliver's head shot up with a surprised look on his face. He had expected a scolding, but instead Grandpa Joseph needed his help. Always eager to please, Oliver quickly agreed to help his grandfather.

Grandpa and Oliver headed out to the garage to sort through lights and get a ladder. Grandpa Joseph explained to Oliver that he would climb the ladder to hang the lights. Oliver's job would be to stay on the ground and pass the lights up to him.

Sitting beside the boxes of Christmas lights was an unopened box that had just recently joined the holiday decorations.

"What's this box, Grandpa?" Oliver asked.

"Oh, your grandmother just bought one of those blow up snowman to put in the front yard," Grandpa Joseph explained.

"Can we set it up?" Oliver asked.

Grandpa Joseph hadn't planned on setting the snowman up yet, but as he stopped to contemplate it, he couldn't determine a reason not to. And if it would make Oliver happy, then why not do it.

"Why, sure we can, Oliver," he said cheerfully. "I will have to get an extension cord and everything we need to blow it up. But there's no reason we can't set it up now."

Grandpa Joseph gathered the necessities to inflate

the snowman, then stood back and watched in glee at the excitement on his grandson's face as the snowman began to take shape. He decided this was a good investment and would have to tell Grandma Mary what a difference it had made for their awkward grandson.

Once the snowman had fully inflated, Joseph returned his attention to the task of hanging lights on the house. He climbed up the ladder and began stapling the lights in place. All seemed to be going very well. Oliver was chattering away, telling Grandpa all about school, while he untangled strings of lights and passed them up to him. Joseph smiled to himself, feeling pleased that he had finally found a task to help build Oliver's self-confidence. All was going well, until Buzzy showed up.

"Grandpa," said Oliver nervously from his position on the ground, "there's a stray dog coming."

Grandpa Joseph glanced nonchalantly over his shoulder and saw Buzzy making his way down the road, heading in their direction. Buzzy seemed unaware of the pair hanging lights on the house. He was more interested in sniffing the newly fallen snow and desecrating on it. But from Oliver's perspective, Buzzy was sniffing him out, tracking his trail with the intent of doing bodily harm to him.

"Grandpa," Oliver said, more nervously and fidgety than before, "he's coming right at me!"

Grandpa Joseph glanced down again, but still didn't see anything to be concerned about. From his bird's eye view, Buzzy just seemed to be in his normal investigative mode. It didn't appear that he was even aware that he was not alone in the yard.

"It's fine, Oliver," Grandpa reassured him. "That's just Buzzy. He's the neighborhood dog that wanders from house to house. He's harmless. Just don't pay any attention to him and he will go away."

But even as he spoke, he could tell Oliver wasn't listening to him. He tried to reassure him that all was fine, but Oliver became more agitated by the moment. And then he started backing toward the house.

"Oliver, stay focused," Grandpa Joseph tried to call him back to the task at hand. "We are hanging lights here, Oliver," he called, when he failed to gain a response from him.

But Oliver's focus remained solely and intently on Buzzy. Since Grandpa Joseph could not seem to break Oliver's focus on Buzzy, he decided it was time for Buzzy to leave.

"Buzzy," he called, trying to get the dog's attention. "Go away!" He couldn't tell him to go home, because Buzzy didn't have a home. "Shoo, Buzzy!" he tried again.

But Buzzy paid no attention to the pair of humans in the yard. He was totally absorbed in the new fallen snow, as if it was his responsibility alone to add color to every inch of the Davis yard.

And then, Buzzy, as if just coming out of a trance and realizing someone had called his name, lifted his head and looked squarely at Oliver. To Grandpa Joseph, it was a look of surprise, with Buzzy just realizing that he was not alone. But to Oliver, it was the look of death. He was sure Buzzy was glaring at him, like he was a piece of meat and he hadn't eaten for weeks.

That's all it took to scare the wits out of Oliver. He completely forgot the task at hand. All he wanted was the safety of the house, and to have a wall of security between him and the man-eating bulldog. He set off in a run for the house, forgetting that he still held the string of lights in his hand. Unfortunately, the other end was located in Grandpa Joseph's hand, and he was still standing at the top of the ladder.

Foreseeing the disaster about to happen, Grandpa Joseph called, "Oliver, let go of the lights!"

Amazingly enough, through his state of panic, Oliver managed to hear and respond to his grandfather's request. But before Grandpa Joseph could breathe a sigh of relief, Oliver's foot got caught in the same string of lights and he tumbled to the floor of the garage. He quickly struggled to his feet, sure that Buzzy was right behind him, and gave the string of lights a quick yank to separate them from his foot. That quick yank was all it took to dislodge Grandpa Joseph from his perch at the top of the ladder.

Oliver, in his flight, made it safely into the house while Grandpa Joseph took a less than graceful flight of his own. He twirled through the air like a giant snowflake, amidst a myriad of baby snowflakes following him from the rooftop. He crash landed directly on top of the newly inflated snowman sitting on the front lawn. There was a horrific bang, sounding almost too loud to be a gunshot and more likely that of a cannon, and then the grandfather and the dead snowman hit the ground simultaneously.

From inside the house, Grandma Mary and Beau heard the loud bang. At the same time, Oliver had charged into the house in a panic-stricken haze, too upset to talk sensibly. All he could utter was one syllable words - "house, lights, buzz…"

Trying to make sense of the combination of words, Mary had come to the conclusion that Grandpa Joseph must have been electrocuted while hanging the lights. But what had caused the bang? Maybe it was a drive by shooting. She and Beau quickly raced out the door while Oliver watched though the window from the safety of the interior of the house. They found Grandpa Joseph lying on the front lawn, simply staring at the vastness of the sky above him, with a background of wrinkled white vinyl located beneath him.

"Joseph," Mary cried in a panic. "Are you okay?"

Grandpa Joseph grunted and said, "I think so, but I haven't tried to get up yet."

"What happened, Dad?" asked Beau, trying to help his father to his feet.

"Did you get zapped?" Mary asked. "Oliver said something about a 'buzz.'"

Grandpa Joseph slowly stood to his feet, bending over to brush himself off. He was about to tell them of another one of Oliver's mishaps when he glanced up and saw the boy watching them from the living room window. His expression was a mixture of lingering fear, along with concern and a measure of defeat stirred in. How could Grandpa Joseph make him feel worse? So he changed his response.

"Oliver and I were having fun hanging the lights," he began, "but the fresh snow looked so inviting, we decided to make some snow angels."

"Oh," said Mom, looking at the sheet of white vinyl under her husband. "That doesn't look much like an angel. What is this big plastic sheet?"

"Oh that," Grandpa Joseph said apprehensively, wiggling his fingers and straightening his legs to make sure nothing was broken.

"That would be what's left of your new inflatable snowman," he explained gingerly.

"But it's flat," Grandma Mary commented, still not quite sure what had just happened.

"That is true," said Joseph, not sure how to proceed with the explanation, still aware of Oliver watching them from the window.

"You blew my snowman up?!" Grandma Mary asked, incredulously.

Beau had been scouting out the situation, and had already figured out what had happened. He could see the tipped ladder and lights hanging from the front of the house, and he had spotted Buzzy nonchalantly walking off down the street.

"So let me guess," he offered his explanation. "You were at the top of the ladder. Oliver was holding the lights, and Buzzy happened along. I know how afraid of dogs Oliver is. So, he probably ran away from the dog, but forgot to let go of the lights."

"Almost right," Grandpa Joseph corrected him. "He did let go of the lights, but then he got his foot caught in the end of the string on the ground and tripped over them. That's what threw me off balance."

"So you fell and landed on my snowman," Grandma Mary stated. From her tone of voice, neither male could determine if she was scolding or just questioning him.

"He saved my life," Grandpa Joseph joked.

"That's right," Beau backed him up. "And what's cheaper, replacing a dead inflatable snowman, or a trip to the emergency room?!"

Mary realized they were right, and the trio chuckled as they made their way through the garage and back into the house. They joked about what a rough day the poor snowman was having. Maybe they had a few broken ornaments, a broken shovel handle, and Grandpa Joseph now had some aches and pains, but at least they weren't flat out on the front lawn.

"He sure got the wind knocked out of him," Beau said, laughing. The rest of the group joined in the laughter and returned to the house to reassure Oliver that all was well.

****

Amazingly enough, the rest of Beau's day was without incidence. The men, along with Oliver, played some board games while Grandma Mary prepared a home-cooked meal. They had an enjoyable time chatting around the dinner table, and then Grandma Mary packed leftovers to send home with her two bachelors.

"Who is coming tomorrow?" Beau asked, on his way to the door.

"Your brother, Joey, is on the agenda," Mary informed him. "He is shipping out after his visit with us."

"Give him our love," Beau told his parents. "It must be hard for him this year. This will be his first Christmas without Christine. It's too bad they couldn't have worked things out."

"She was just tired of following him around," said Mary, trying to find a sense of reason for the recent divorce.

Beau nodded, knowing the pain of divorce. "Thanks for a wonderful day," he simply said, giving his parents one last hug.

Oliver smiled up at his grandmother and said, "Sorry

about ripping your sign, and breaking the ornaments.”

Looking at Grandpa Joseph, he added, “And sorry I broke your shovel, and that you fell off the ladder, and that the snowman blew up.”

“Don’t you worry about it,” both grandparents chorused.

“Those were old ornaments anyway,” Grandma Mary said, giving her grandson a hug. “It’s time to get some new ones. And I can buy a new snowman anytime.”

“Sometimes accidents happen,” added Grandpa Joseph, patting him on the head.

Beau and Oliver exited the house and Mary and Joseph waved goodbye from the living room window.

“Yes, accidents happen….” Grandpa Joseph spoke softly, as he continued to smile and wave, “….and very frequently with a child like Oliver!”

****

****

Joseph

****

Chapter 4
Joseph

✯✯✯✯✯✯✯

Mary decorated the front door with a manger scene, lovingly placing a "Joseph" sign above the father figure. Although he was their third offspring, it was he that bore his father's name.

Mary and Joseph had had their hearts set on producing a daughter. When the third attempt once more proved to be a male, they were at a loss for a masculine name. So he became Joseph, Jr., mostly for lack of another idea.

Joey (as he was soon nicknamed) had chosen a life in the military. He had been married for several years, but now found himself recently divorced. They had failed to produce an offspring, and his wife had tired of rotating between following him from base-to-base or spending time alone awaiting his return.

Finding himself on his own again, and not yet ready for another relationship, Joey had decided to focus more firmly on his military career. And for companionship, he simply invested in a pet bird. It gave him someone to talk to, but didn't require a lifetime commitment from him. He had already made arrangements for his parents to "bird sit" during his deployment. His mother had reluctantly agreed to it, but had warned Joey that she was not good with animals and had no idea how to care for a bird. He had assured her that birds required little attention – just food, water and an occasional conversation. He persuaded her that she could handle it, and that little friend, Banjo, would be no problem whatsoever.

Joseph, Jr. arrived on Day Three in full uniform attire. His mother was always so proud to see him in uniform, and it almost brought her to tears each time. And since he would be shipping out soon, he wanted to impress her one last time before he left.

He pulled into the familiar driveway and stepped out of the car. Walking to the passenger side of the car, he retrieved Banjo to bring him inside to meet his new caregivers. What he didn't notice was that Buzzy was just rounding the snow bank at the end of the driveway.

Looking up, Buzzy's intense search of the snow bank suddenly lost all interest. Only a few feet away stood a man in full uniform, and Buzzy hated uniforms with a passion. He knew he had a job to do, and he wasted no time stepping up to the challenge. He started to snarl, followed by a growl, which quickly erupted into a ferocious bark.

Hearing the fierce sound of barking so close behind him, Joey poked his head out to investigate. It didn't take long for him to realize that he was the focus of the animosity. He didn't know whose dog it was, but it was coming his way - and coming fast! Joey tried briefly to talk the dog down, but Buzzy wasn't interested in talking. He charged straight toward Joey, who quickly retreated into the safety of the house. Joey slammed the door behind him, startling his parents who were sitting comfortably in the living room.

"Joey!" Mom cried, jumping up to greet him. "I didn't realize you were here."

"Whose ferocious dog is that?" Joey asked.

Dad looked out the window, and Buzzy was still vehemently barking at the front door.

"Oh, that's just Buzzy, the neighborhood dog," he explained.

"Well, he's not too friendly for a neighborhood dog," Joey argued. "He looked like he wanted to take my leg off."

Dad shook his head in agreement and added, "Buzzy hates uniforms. The mailman has a terrible time with him, too. It would be nice if they let him wear street clothes!"

The elder Joseph walked to the front door and opening it, he simply scolded, "That's enough, Buzzy. It's time to move on."

Buzzy obediently stopped barking and turned to walk away. He appeared to immediately forget the whole episode, resuming his exploration of the new snow banks.

"I didn't even have time to get Banjo out of the car," Joey said. "Buzzy came at me with full force, and I thought it was best to just retreat. I think I'd rather be on the front line than to face that dog again. I'm not sure I want to go back out there."

"I'll go get him for you, son," his father volunteered.

"Thanks, Dad," said Joey. "He's in his cage on the front seat. He chatted my ear off all the way over here."

Joseph, Sr. headed out the door to retrieve Banjo from the car. He opened the passenger door and greeted the little bird.

"Hello there, little guy," he said cheerfully. "You are going to be our houseguest for awhile." He poked a finger in the cage to try to pet the bird, and Banjo immediately pecked him.

"Ow!" Dad cried, quickly retreating from the cage. "We are not off to a good start here, son. I hope you are not going to be a challenge."

The senior Joseph carried Banjo into the house and handed the cage to his proud owner.

"Mom and Dad," Joey said, looking much like a proud father, "meet Banjo."

"I already did," said Dad, studying his bruised finger.

"Did he bite you?" Joey asked.

"Just a little nip," Dad responded.

"Banjo," Joey scolded the little bird, "you need to be nice to your grandfather. He's going to be taking care of you for awhile. Don't you know you should never bite the hand that feeds you?"

Banjo just tweeted in his cage, oblivious to the lecture from his owner. Mom smiled at the innocent-looking bird and came to give her son a hug.

"It's so good to see you, sweetie," she said. "Come on into the kitchen and I'll make you a cup of coffee."

Joey obediently followed his mother into the kitchen, bird cage still in hand, followed by his father who was keeping an eye on the innocent-looking bird, wondering what kind of trouble he would cause. Arriving in the kitchen, Joey none too gently plopped the bird cage on top of Dad's brand new island. Dad winced, almost feeling the pain as if Joey had dropped the cage on his big toe, and worried about what kind of damage the cage might have caused.

Mom conversed freely as she made cups of coffee for the group. Joey responded appropriately, but it was quite evident that his focus was fixed on Banjo. Mom turned to hand Joey his cup of coffee just as he opened the cage door.

"You're not going to take him out, are you, Joseph?" she demanded.

"Sure I am," he eagerly responded. "He spends a lot of time flying freely around my place."

"We don't want him loose here, though, son," Dad commented.

"I won't let him get away, Dad," Joey promised. "He sits on my shoulder all the time and doesn't give me a hard time about getting back in the cage. Just watch and see."

To prove how well behaved Banjo was, he perched him on his shoulder. Banjo gave him a delicate peck on the ear and rubbed his head against his chin. Then he sat back and chirped.

Joey chuckled and said, "See how comfortable he is? We do this all the time."

Grabbing the bird cage, he dragged it off the counter and said, "Where do you want me to put this?"

Dad winced again, not daring to look at his countertop. Mom and Joey headed to the den, apparently not noticing the freshly carved groove, while Dad lingered behind to inspect the damage.

"Nothing lasts forever," he muttered to himself, "but I was hoping it would last a little longer than a month!"

Joseph, Sr. shrugged his shoulders, accepting his fate, and wandered into the den to find his wife and namesake. They were placing the cage on top of one of his bookshelves, discussing how Banjo would be comfortable in his new temporary location.

"Are you sure he's okay on your shoulder?" Mom asked, still concerned that he might take flight or, even worse, desecrate of Joey's uniform.

"He's fine, Mom," Joey insisted.

"What if he has to go to the bathroom?" she persisted. "I don't want him to leave droppings on my furniture, or your uniform."

Joseph, Jr. smiled at his mother and gave her a reassuring hug. "He never has, Mom. He's smart enough to fly back into his cage when he has to go."

Trusting her son, Mom smiled and said, "Well in that case, let's sit down and visit for awhile."

Mom, Dad and their third offspring settled on the sofas and chatted about old times, current happenings, and plans for the future. Joey was sharing some details about his upcoming deployment and all was going well, until the cuckoo clock started to chime. When the cuckoo bird came out to announce the hour, the sleepy, little, mellow bird resting calmly on Joey's shoulder suddenly came to life.

He took flight with such force that he left a stream of bird poop across the back of Mom's couch. She gasped in horror and was surprised to hear her son chuckle. This was not a laughing matter. She looked up, ready to reprimand him for keeping the bird out of his cage for so long, when she noticed the source of his humor. Little Banjo was almost flying circles around the cuckoo bird as it popped in and out of the house announcing each hour.

"That's kind of cute," Dad commented, handing Mom some tissues as she tried to quickly swab the bird poop off her sofa.

"Cute!" Joey guffawed, "I think it's hysterical!" He chuckled again, as if to prove his point.

Banjo continued his attempt to catch the cuckoo bird, and seemed dejected when it finally retreated back inside the house. He perched himself on top of the cuckoo clock and leaned forward to watch the door, waiting for the little bird to reappear.

"Come on, Banjo," Joey coaxed, "time to get back into your cage."

But Banjo apparently had no intention of moving. He seemed content to remain on the peak of the clock, waiting for the return of his soul-mate. Mom and Dad joined their son in the quest to catch his little feathered friend, but nothing they did could coax him into coming down.

"I have a net," Dad suggested, remembering his supplies in the garage. "It's a fishing net, but I think it would work if you want to try to catch him."

"I'm not sure I need a net," Joey said, "but you can get it if you want. I'm just gonna pull a chair over and try to reach him while I'm waiting. He's not usually this difficult to catch."

"Well, you don't have a beautiful cuckoo bird at your place," Mom chuckled.

Dad headed for the garage to retrieve his net while Joey continued the mission of retrieving his bird. However, nothing he said or did could convince little Banjo to abandon his post. He was a love-struck canary, waiting for his heart-throb to return.

"I can't get him," Joey sighed in exasperation.

He sat down on the couch beside his mother to await his father's return. When it appeared that Joseph, Sr. had been gone longer than it should have taken to retrieve a net, his namesake decided to go check on him.

He found him shuffling around in an excessive amount of clutter in the garage. Seeing Joey enter, Dad looked up to address him.

"As organized as I have become in my retirement, I just haven't had the ambition to take on this garage yet," he paused and sighed. "I thought I could put my hands right on that net, but I can't seem to locate it anywhere."

The two men poked and prodded, moving objects here and there in an effort to find the missing net. It seemed each item they found triggered a memory or a story.

"Hey, look at all the fishing poles!" Joey said excitedly,

when he discovered several of them standing in the corner.

He stopped to explore each one, his mind full of memories of fishing days with his father and brothers.

Locating his pole, he said, "This one is mine. I remember when you bought it for me on my eighth birthday."

He smiled up at his father and said, "That was the best birthday present ever. I had a lot of fun with this pole."

The two men smiled, their eyes distant, while fishing memories floated around in their heads. Then returning to the poles, Dad picked one up and investigated it a little closer.

"Whose pole is this?" he asked, trying to connect his sons with their poles.

Joey chuckled. "That one was Berry's," he smiled. Pointing at the handle, he added, "Remember how he carved a 'B' in it so everyone would know it was his? He forgot 'Beau' starts with a B, too!"

Dad and Joey got to reminiscing about fishing expeditions, and completely forgot the task of finding the net. When neither of the men returned, Mary became concerned and came to join them in the garage.

"What's happening out here?" she asked, stepping through the doorway.

"I can't seem to find my fishing net," he husband explained, looking up at her with his pole still in his hands.

"Well, that's obviously not it," she smiled at him. Pointing to the wall on the other side of the garage, she added, "But that looks like it over there."

The men looked toward the wall where she was pointing, then back at each other. They grinned and shook their heads. All the time they had just spent searching, and Mary had spotted the net in no time.

They looked at her in amazement. She just shrugged and said, "I think you men were just looking too hard."

Joey went to retrieve the net off the wall, and added, "Or having too much fun remembering the good old days."

"That we were," Dad agreed, looking fondly toward his wife.

"Well, there's nothing wrong with that," Mom smiled back at him.

Walking back across the garage, Joey asked, "What was Banjo doing when you left him?"

"Still sitting on top of the clock," she replied. "He almost looked like he was falling asleep."

Joey chuckled. "He's probably tired of waiting for his girlfriend to return."

The trio returned to the den, and Mom looked anxiously at the clock. The love struck bird was still perched on top of it. Joey approached with the net, trying to find the right angle to attempt to retrieve Banjo.

"Just be careful of my cuckoo clock. Dad bought that for me when we were in Germany," she reminded him.

Looking at the time, she added, "Maybe you should wait. It's getting close to the hour and the cuckoo bird will be coming out soon."

"I've got time, Mom," Joey insisted. "It will just take me a second."

He climbed back into Dad's recliner and positioned himself, net in hand. It momentarily looked like everything was going to work out fine, but then disaster struck. Just as he swung the net to catch his fine-feathered friend, the cuckoo clock came to life again and Banjo went crazy. Joey's swing was already in motion and caught the little cuckoo bird by force. It not only knocked him off his perch, but took the whole perch with him.

Joey looked into the net with horror clearly displayed across his face. Banjo still fluttered freely around the cuckoo clock, desperately trying to find his statue girlfriend. Joey gingerly reached into his net, and slowly pulled out Mom's cuckoo bird. It was still intact and attached to its perch, but now completely severed from its home on the wall. The clock was still chiming out the hour, but now bird-free.

"My clock!!" Mom gasped, dropping down onto the couch and covering her face with her hands. "It made it safely all the way home from Germany only to get broken in my own living room!"

"Joseph…." Dad started, in a reprimanding voice, but hesitated when he saw the look on his son's face. It was all a very unfortunate accident, so Dad decided instead to comfort his distraught wife on the couch.

Joseph, Jr. felt absolutely terrible. His special day with his parents on the day before his departure back to the base, and he had ruined it by destroying one of his mother's prize possessions. He felt like an awkward school boy again, and sat slowly down on the couch beside his mother. He knew nothing he could say could make her feel better. She was right. The clock had traveled safely across half the globe, and then he had foolishly destroyed it while trying to rescue his out-of-control bird. He felt like his mother should just spank him and send him to his room, as if that would really solve anything.

"I'm so sorry, Mom," he said softly, wishing there was something he could do to rectify the situation. He held the cuckoo bird up and inspected it. "It looks like a clean break," he said. "Maybe Dad can fix it."

Dad shrugged and said, "It's possible."

He reached out a hand to take the cuckoo bird for a closer inspection. But before Joey could hand it to him, Banjo flew off his perch on the clock and came down to rest on the broken perch beside the tiny cuckoo bird.

As hopeless as the situation seemed, the trio burst into laughter at the canary's antics. He was head-over-heels (or beak-over-tail) in love with the wooden cuckoo bird glued to its wooden perch.

"You are a trouble-maker, Banjo," Joey chuckled, as he tenderly rubbed his head. "I better put you back in your cage before you cause any more problems."

He handed the cuckoo bird to his father and picked Banjo up to return him to his cage. But as he turned to walk away, Banjo went berserk and started pecking at his hands.

"Ow," Joey cried. "Banjo, what is wrong with you? You don't usually behave like this."

Not able to bear the pecking of his sharp beak, Joey released Banjo, who immediately flew back to the cuckoo bird.

Joey tried several times to retrieve Banjo and return him to his cage, but the same scenario played out each time, with Banjo winning out and flying back to roost beside the cuckoo bird.

"This is nuts," Joey muttered.

"But kind of comical," Mom smiled.

Joey was glad to see his mother smile. He felt absolutely terrible for having broken her clock, but at least she was able to smile again.

"What should I do?" Joey asked, looking at his parents for guidance. "I can't get Banjo back in his cage because he doesn't want to leave the cuckoo bird."

"Just put the cuckoo bird in the cage with him," Mom suggested.

Dad raised an eyebrow and asked, "Are you sure?"

"Will he hurt it?" she questioned.

Joey shrugged a shoulder and said, "I'm not really sure. I've never put any objects in his cage before. But he seems to just want to be with the cuckoo, not hurt it. If he is in love with it, I doubt he would do any damage to it."

"Well, I guess it can't hurt to try," Mom said. "We have to get him back in his cage somehow. He can't fly loose around the house."

Dad piped up and said, "We'll just keep an eye on him. If the cuckoo bird starts to show any signs of abuse, we'll just take it out of the cage."

With Mom and Dad in agreement, Joey retrieved Banjo (along with his cuckoo bird girlfriend) and returned him to his cage. Banjo looked happy as a lark, sitting beside his newfound love, chirping happily away. Mom and Joey chuckled, and Dad shook his head in disbelief.

"Who would have thought a live canary would be so crazy about a wooden cuckoo bird," Dad said.

Mom decided it was time for lunch, so the group moved

into the kitchen. The remainder of Joey's day proved to be an enjoyable time of family fun. It still broke Mom's heart every time the cuckoo clock chimed and the door opened to reveal an empty nest, but perhaps Dad would be able to repair it sometime in the near future.

"Who comes tomorrow?" Joey inquired.

"Noel is coming with her family," Mom informed him.

"Cassandra and Spencer must be getting big," Joey commented.

"Oh, yes," said Dad, "and quite lively."

"Spencer is seven and can be quite a handful," Mom said. "And Cassandra is getting all grown up. She will be a teenager in just a couple of years."

Joey took on a momentary look of sadness and said, "It's the kids I miss the most when I'm gone. They grow up so fast, and I don't like missing out on their childhood."

Mom tried to encourage him by reminding him that there were a lot of ways to communicate, and everyone was good about keeping in touch. Joey knew this to be true, but pictures and emails were not the same as being there.

With the day drawing to a close, Joey decided it was time for him to say goodbye. He gave Banjo a brief talk, reminding him to behave for his grandparents while he was away.

After hugs and kisses for Mom and Dad, Joey headed out to his car. Unfortunately, Buzzy was waiting for him in the front yard. One glance at the military uniform, and Buzzy was in hot pursuit.

Joseph, Jr. made it successfully to his car, hopping in before Buzzy could grasp hold of his pant leg. He backed his car out of the yard, pulled around in front of the house, and stopped to call out a final goodbye to his parents.

Rolling down his window, he called, "I won that battle and got to the car before he did!"

His parents smiled and Dad gave him a thumb's up.

"Now, if I can just be as successful in the real battle," Joey jokingly called out.

"You'll do just fine, son," his Dad called back. "You're a smart boy."

"Stay safe, sweetie!" Mom called to him, blowing her son a kiss for luck.

Just then Buzzy came running up to the car, still barking ferociously.

"He doesn't give up, does he?!" Joey laughed.

He waved goodbye, stepped on the throttle and sped off down the road, with Buzzy still chasing him. Off they went, around the corner and out of sight - the military man off to battle, and the ferocious neighborhood dog hot on his trail, looking much like a heat-seeking missile.

****

****

Noel

****

Chapter 5
Noel

✫✫✫✫✫✫✫

The next morning the Davis family awoke to a fresh coat of snow. Fortunately, it was not enough to interrupt plans, and Noel arrived with her family on Day Four as scheduled. Mom had left the manger scene on the door, but had removed the "Joseph" sign and replaced it with a sign stating "The First (and only) Noel."

Noel stopped at the front door long enough to take note of her mother's creativity. Smiling, she kicked the new-fallen snow off her boots, opened the door, and called out, "We're here!"

"Oh, Noel, you made it," Mom said, as she rushed to greet the newcomers. "Thank goodness the storm wasn't worse."

"Well, it's not like we had far to go," chuckled Noel's husband, Brent. He gave Mary a hug and continued, "We just live a few blocks away, you know."

"Yeah, and we could have walked if we wanted to," Spencer piped up, taking off his hat and mittens.

"Oh, you guys," Grandma Mary said, giving them a big hug. "I'm so glad you're here. We are going to have a fun day today."

Grandma Mary was helping Spencer and Cassandra take off their coats and hang them up when Grandpa Joseph came into the room.

"Hey, where are my hugs?" he asked.

"Grandpa!" both kids chorused, running to shower him with hugs.

"I brought something to show you, Grandpa," Spencer said, heading back to the front door to retrieve the new fishing pole he had brought with him. "Look what my dad just gave me!" he said excitedly.

"Wow! A new pole," Grandpa Joseph said, turning it over in his hands as he examined it. "When spring comes, I'll take you fishing and show you how to cast."

"Oh, I already know how," Spencer eagerly replied. "Just watch this!"

All four adults started to protest, but Spencer was faster than words. Before anyone could stop him, he swung his fishing pole back and set his cast into motion. Unfortunately, he was standing too close to the Christmas tree. Not only did his pole strike the tree, but his line became entangled in a branch. His thrust toppled the tree and sent it crashing to the floor.

"Spencer!" Noel said in a hoarse whisper, her mouth open in disbelief.

"Didn't I tell you fishing poles are not for indoor use?" Brent scolded his son. "You haven't even been here five minutes and you have already created a disaster! I think you need to take a time-out, but apologize to your grandparents first."

Spencer was close to tears and Grandma Mary feared the day would be ruined before it got started. Trying to salvage the situation, she said, "Grandpa, why don't you take Spencer into your library and show him Joey's bird. We'll clean this mess up. We will just need a little help standing the tree back up."

Spencer gave his grandmother a hug and told her how sorry he was. Grandpa Joseph ushered him off to the library while Brent helped to upright the tree. Noel, her mother, and Cassandra set to work redecorating the tree.

"He's such a handful, Mom," Noel complained. "I haven't cleaned up one mess and he's already into another. He has been that way all his life. I was hoping things would improve as he got older, but it hasn't happened yet. He totally wears me out!"

"He's just an adventurous boy, Noel," her mother reassured her. "Your brothers were the same way, and so isn't Beau's son, Oliver. As hard as it seems right now, you'll get through it. You've got a good husband to support you." Looking at Cassandra, she added, "And a wonderful daughter, too."

Noel brightened and said, "Cassandra is getting so grown up. She's learning to bake and sew - oh, Cassandra," Noel paused. "You brought your gifts for Grammy and Grampy, right?."

In their chaotic entrance, Cassandra's gifts had been forgotten in the hallway. Her grandmother said, "Oh, sweetie, why don't you go get them. I can fix this old tree later."

Cassandra went to retrieve the gifts, and Grandma Mary suggested they go join the men in the library.

"Grandpa," Mary called to her husband, as they entered the library. "Cassandra brought some presents for us."

Cassandra carried her gifts, beaming from ear-to-ear. Taking one present at a time from her bag, she handed them to her grandparents and said, "I made these all by myself."

Her grandparents accepted their gifts with a chorus of "Thank you's."

Grandpa Joseph was the first to unwrap his gift and held up a loosely knit neon green vest. He tried to hide his surprise at such a brilliant color. Recovering quickly, he looked up and said, "You made this, sweetie?"

Cassandra bobbed her head affirmatively, grinning with pride. "Mom taught me to knit and this is my first project."

Grandpa Joseph got up and gave her a hug. "Well, I am truly honored to be the recipient of your first knitting project. Thank you, honey!"

"Put it on to see if it fits," suggested Spencer.

"Okay," said Grandpa, "I can do that."

He pulled the vest over his head and turned around to model it for everyone.

"You did a good job, Cassandra," Noel complimented her daughter. "It's a perfect fit."

Cassandra turned her attention to her grandmother and anxiously said, "Okay, Grammy, open yours now."

Grandma Mary unwrapped her gift, then stood up to display a bright red apron covered with huge sunflowers and lined with frilly yellow lacing.

"I didn't realize you could sew, sweetie," she said.

Cassandra smiled and explained that this was the first project she had made with her youth group through the church.

"So try yours on, too, Grammy," Spencer insisted.

Grandma Mary was quick to oblige, thanking Cassandra for thinking of her. Noel explained that Cassandra had been learning lots of new things through her involvement with the youth group, including skills like knitting, sewing and cooking. Spencer had joined, too. They had a special unit for boys and would have a fishing derby in the spring, which is why his father had bought him a new fishing pole.

"You kids are growing up so fast," Grandma Mary commented. "Your grandfather and I couldn't be prouder of you."

"So what should we do today?" Grandpa Joseph asked, moving on to plans of the day.

"Well, Cassandra has an idea," Noel said, hesitantly. When Grandma Mary looked at her questioningly, she continued. "Cassandra learned to make éclairs and wanted to bake some for you."

"I just love to bake," Cassandra smiled at her grandmother. "Can I show you how it's done?"

"Okay," Grandma Mary agreed. "The girls can hang out in the kitchen. So what will the boys do?"

"Can I watch Joey's bird some more?" Spencer asked. "I always wanted a bird, but Mom says I'm not ready for a pet yet. She thinks I need to learn to be more responsible."

"That's fine, Spencer," Grandpa Joseph spoke up. "Just don't put your fingers in the cage. Banjo is not afraid to bite." Looking at his bruised finger, he added, "I found that out the hard way."

The ladies headed for the kitchen and Joseph took Brent off to show him all the accomplishments he had made during his first few months of retirement. Brent, knowing how mischievous his son could be, and not convinced that leaving him with the bird was a good idea, called over his shoulder, "Spencer, if you get bored, you can either come find Grandpa Joseph and me, or go join your mother in the kitchen."

Once in the kitchen, Noel and her mother settled on the stools at the new island Grandpa Joseph had built, while Cassandra sprang into action. She was anxious to show her grandmother her newfound cooking skills.

"Okay," she started, as if teaching her very own cooking class, "Today, we are going to make chocolate éclairs. I brought my own recipe with me."

She reached into her pocket, pulled out the recipe and began reading off the list of ingredients. When she got to vanilla pudding, Grandma Mary spoke up.

"I don't think I have any vanilla pudding, sweetie," she informed her.

"Oh, this is a quick recipe," Noel explained. "It uses pudding for the filling instead of making it from scratch."

"Well, that's not a problem," Grandma Mary assured them, putting her problem solving skills to work. "You two can get started, and I'll just run to the store to buy some."

"You don't mind, Mom?" Noel asked. "We don't want to be an inconvenience."

"Not at all," her mother reassured her. "It will only take a few minutes. I'll just go to the convenience store on the corner. The pudding may cost a few cents more, but I don't want to waste anymore of our precious time together than I have to."

"Thanks, Grandma," Cassandra smiled at her grandmother. "You're the best!"

Grandma Mary gave her granddaughter a quick hug and headed out the door, thinking to herself, I try to be! She grabbed her car keys and was throwing on a coat as she walked by the living room, where Joseph was showing Brent their souvenirs from their European trip. She explained that she was just taking a quick trip to the store, but didn't stop to contemplate the odd look that Joseph gave her.

****

Mary quickly rushed to the most convenient store. She had only one day with Noel and her family, and wanted to spend as much time with them as possible. But as fate would have it, she bumped into Mrs. Margaret Wellington, who was out on a quick errand herself.

Margaret was a devout member of the church that Mary and Joseph attended, and also had her hand in almost every committee in town. She was the leader of the ladies' group at church, as well as president of the community organization named Project CARE. The organization had been formed to help families in need, thus the acronym CARE stood for Collection and Redistribution of Enfield. The organization would accept donations and find needy families and children to redistribute them to.

While the organization was good and necessary, it wasn't necessarily good that Margaret had been made the president. The position had gone straight to her head, and made her feel like she stood a head taller than everyone else. The irony of the situation was that Margaret Wellington, of all people, had no clue what it was like to be a person in need. But her rank and power had aided her in laying claim to the position as president. She constantly referred to this project as "her baby," and frequently reminded other committee members of how important a role she played. Why if it wasn't for her insight and generosity, she would tell them, this organization would cease to exist.

As usual, she was the last person Mary wanted to run into, especially when she was in a hurry.

"Well, Mary," Margaret called out cheerfully. "It's so good to see you."

Mary groaned internally. She had tried to duck behind a display of potato chips before Margaret could spot her, but her efforts had been unsuccessful.

"Oh, Margaret," Mary smiled in return, putting on her best possible charm. "It's good to see you, too."

Mary knew it wasn't polite to lie, but on the other hand, she was too polite to say what she was really thinking. Plus, she didn't like to intentionally cause another person discomfort, no matter how much she disliked them.

"Are you here alone?" Margaret questioned, looking around.

Mary grit her teeth. Margaret Wellington made little effort to hide her attraction toward Mary's husband. She openly flirted with him, and always sought him out at church services. Joseph paid little heed to her, and did nothing to encourage her attentions, but Margaret didn't seem to notice. She simply continued to try to charm him with her womanly mannerisms, oblivious to the fact that he appeared to be a happily married man with twelve children.

Mary had little time or desire for small talk, so she quickly and politely explained that Joseph was home entertaining Noel and her family, and that she needed to get back as soon as possible. Mary grabbed a box of vanilla pudding and turned to find Margaret staring disdainfully at her again.

There she is, looking down her nose at me like usual, Mary thought to herself. *Who does she think she is to look at me that way? She always thinks she is so much better than everyone else.*

Mary politely excused herself and hurried to check out so she could rejoin her family. When she got back to the house, Joseph met her in the entry way and helped her take her coat off.

"Did you really wear that to the store?" he asked, looking down at her brightly-colored, frilly apron, which had been clearly visible beneath her unbuttoned coat.

"Oh, no," Mary gasped. "I forgot I had it on. Why didn't you say something?"

"And risk Cassandra hearing me?" he questioned. "I didn't want her to think you didn't like her gift."

"That's true," Mary agreed, and then gasped again. "I

bumped into Margaret Wellington at the store. No wonder she looked at me like she did!"

She paused, then added over her shoulder as she headed back to the kitchen, "Oh, well! It will give her something to talk about."

Joseph chuckled and went to rejoin Brent so they could finish the tour of the house. Mom and Noel had a good time chatting while Cassandra demonstrated her baking skills. She baked her éclairs and the two ladies helped her fill them with the vanilla pudding. Then it was time to make the chocolate frosting. However, Cassandra had never used a propane kitchen stove before. When she lit the burner on the top of the stove, it startled her and she let out a scream.

Spencer, hearing her scream from the other room, came running to investigate. He had never seen a propane kitchen stove either, and immediately assumed the top of the stove was on fire. Realizing he was the only "man" in the kitchen, he decided it was up to him to handle this emergency. He quickly grabbed Grandma Mary's fire extinguisher sitting on the counter and doused the fire.

Feeling very proud of himself for reacting so quickly, he turned to his mother and said, "Did you see that, Mom? I put the fire out!!!"

All three females simply stood there, staring open-mouthed at the mess that covered the top of Grandma Mary's kitchen stove. Noel could only nod her head in the affirmative, not quite sure what to say next.

Hearing all the commotion coming from the kitchen, Grandpa Joseph and Brent came hurrying in.

"What happened?" asked Grandpa Joseph.

"Spencer put the fire out," Noel said weakly.

"You had a kitchen fire?" Brent asked.

"Sort of...," Grandma Mary said.

Cassandra still stood near the stove, wearing a shocked expression and looking like she would cry at any moment.

"I used the fire extinguisher just like you taught me, Daddy," Spencer beamed proudly. "Pull the pin and then sweep the hose from side-to-side!"

Brent returned only a half-smile to his son. He still hadn't determined what had just happened. He was glad Spencer knew how to use a fire extinguisher, but he wasn't convinced the situation had warranted it. Everyone stood in an awkward silence, not sure of what to do next.

Once again, it was Grandma Mary who came to the rescue to save the day. Thinking fast, she said, "You know, Cassandra, I can frost the éclairs later. And this mess can wait. Why don't we all go out and get some pizza?"

Everyone was anxious to get out of the current situation and quickly agreed that pizza sounded like a good idea. Grandma Mary went to grab her coat again, but as she walked by the library, something caught her eye. Spencer's fishing pole was leaning against the bird cage. Knowing he wouldn't want to leave it behind, she went to retrieve it for him. However, when she got to the bird cage, she realized that Joey's bird was lying motionless on the bottom of the cage. She poked little Banjo with the end of Spencer's fishing pole a couple of times, but the poor bird remained motionless.

"Spencer," she called down the hallway. "What happened to Uncle Joey's bird?"

Spencer stepped sheepishly into the room, quickly followed by his worried mother and still stunned sister.

"I don't really know, Gram," he began. "Grandpa said not to touch him, so I didn't."

"But it looks like he is dead," Grandma Mary continued to question him. "You must have done something to him."

"Well….," Spencer began, "I didn't touch him. I poked him with my fishing pole."

"How many times did you poke him?" Noel demanded of her son.

"Well….," Spencer continued, "he kept pecking at my pole. I had to do something, Mom. He wouldn't let go of my pole."

"So you poked him to death?" she demanded.

"No," Spencer adamantly denied the accusation. "I

shook my pole to try to get him off it, and he hit his head on the cuckoo bird."

Noel looked questioningly at her son, and he hurried on, "I didn't mean to, Mom." Starting to tear up, he added, "It was an accident, honest, it was! I didn't mean to hurt Uncle Joey's bird!"

Wondering where the rest of the gang was, Grandpa Joseph and Brent had come back to look for them. They came into the library just as Spencer was ready to burst into tears.

"What's going on?" Grandpa Joseph asked.

"What you really mean is - What did Spencer do this time?" Brent added.

Grandma Mary put a protective arm around Spencer's shoulders and said, "Spencer is just upset because Uncle Joey's bird died."

Grandpa Joseph raised an eyebrow and looking at his wife, he asked, "You killed Joey's bird already? I know you don't have good luck with pets, but I thought he would last longer than a day."

"So did I," Grandma Mary said, raising an eyebrow of her own. "Now let's go get some pizza."

****

This time, they made it successfully out the door. Loading the family into their vehicles, they headed off to Perry's Pizza to try to forget the trials of the morning. It proved to be a good idea, as all members of the family chatted and joked freely throughout the meal.

When the pizza was gone and the drinks were finished, Grandma Mary asked if Noel wanted to bring her family back to the house for some dessert.

"No, we really should head home," she replied. "We are heading up to spend a few days with Brent's family, and I need to get home and pack a few things." She paused, and then added, "Plus, you have a lot to deal with at your house."

"True on both accounts," Grandma Mary agreed, thinking of the Christmas tree that still needed redecorating, the stovetop that needed cleaning, the éclairs that needed frosting, and what to do with Joey's dead bird?

"And you need to get ready for your company tomorrow, Grandma," Cassandra reminded her grandmother.

"Who's coming tomorrow?" Spencer questioned, thinking this twelve day Christmas plan was a pretty neat idea.

"That would be Gloria," Grandma Mary replied, patting her grandson on the head.

"Is she bringing her crazy mother-in-law?" Brent asked.

"Brent!" Noel quickly reprimanded her husband. "It is not our place to judge."

Mary responded that she imagined Gloria would be bringing Francine with her. Jack didn't like to leave his mother behind.

Noel sighed. "Sometimes I feel overwhelmed with all I have to deal with, but poor Gloria. She really has her hands full with her situation. I guess it's a blessing that she doesn't have kids to deal with, too."

"She's a brave girl, though," Grandpa Joseph came to her defense. "We didn't raise our kids to be cowards. They can handle a challenge." He winked at Noel and she smiled back. Dad always had a way of making her feel brave and strong.

After hugs and kisses, Noel's family piled into their car and waved good-bye.

"Tell Uncle Joey I'm really sorry about his bird," Spencer called from the backseat of the car.

"I will, sweetie," Grandma Mary called back.

After they had driven away, Joseph asked, "How are you going to tell Joey that his bird died?"

Mary just smiled smugly and said, "I'm not. Tomorrow Gloria and I are going shopping. And we are going to bring home a new bird that looks just like little Banjo!"

Joseph chuckled, hugged his wife and gave her a kiss on the head. "You are an amazing woman, do you know that?"

he asked her.

"Of course I do," Mary smiled back. "You can't raise your kids to be brave, strong, and ready to take on a challenge if you aren't brave and strong yourself."

Joseph looked lovingly at his wife and added, "And clever, too!!"

"I think that's why you married me," Mary teased, giving him a quick kiss on the cheek, as she turned and walked away.

****

✷✷✷✷✷✷✷

Gloria

✷✷✷✷✷✷✷

Chapter 6
Gloria

★★★★★★★

Mary woke up exhausted the next morning. She had spent the night frosting éclairs, cleaning the top of her kitchen stove, and putting ornaments back into place on the Christmas tree. And she had done nothing with Joey's dead bird in the library. But she had changed the scene on the front door, replacing the manger scene with a set of musical notes to celebrate Gloria's arrival.

Gloria had married an older man with substance, which had both positive and negative features. On the good side, she was able to travel frequently, had a beautiful home, and luxurious cars to drive. On the down side, she would probably never have children of her own, and it was a package deal which came with a senile mother-in-law to care for.

Many were the nights when she called her mother in tears, just needing a shoulder to cry on. Mary had asked if it might be best to find a good home for Francine, but Gloria's husband, Jack, would not hear of it. He insisted that no one could provide for her better than they could, and he needed to know that she was safe. Plus, he had signed a contract with his mother in her younger years.

When Francine realized she was developing senile dementia, she had formed an agreement with her only son that he would take care of her and not stuff her away in an institution. And Jack was a man who stood by his word, even if his mother was past the point of understanding. So Gloria made the best of it, trying to take one day at a time, knowing that this could not go on forever.

Gloria arrived at the old homestead on Day Five and smiled at the musical notes on the front door. Her mother had always been so creative and knew how to make each child feel loved and special. Gloria chuckled to herself as she thought, My mom keeps up with twelve kids and everything happening in their lives, and I can't even manage one senile old lady!

After rounds of hugs and greetings, Joseph and Jack went to chat in the library. Francine was wandering around the living room, looking at pictures and picking up various items to investigate on a closer scale.

"I don't think she will break anything, Mom," Gloria said, realizing her mother was watching Francine.

"Oh, there's not much here that I am worried about anyway," Mary replied. "Just my Tiffany lamp and the vase from Vienna. Joey already broke my cuckoo clock."

Gloria gasped, and her mother recounted the story of Joey and his loose bird.

"That is so sad, Mom," Gloria sighed. "I know how excited you were about that clock."

Mary remained upbeat. "After the holidays are over, your father is going to work on it and see if he can fix it. But right now, I have a bigger problem to deal with."

Pointing toward the library where the bird cage sat, she continued, "Spencer accidentally killed Joey's bird yesterday."

Gloria covered her mouth with her hand and said, "Oh, no! How did he manage to do that? Joey loves that little bird."

Mary explained how Spencer had a new fishing pole that he was protective of and Joey's bird wouldn't let go of it. When the battle was finished, the fishing pole came out the winner. And now poor little Banjo was gone.

"So what are you going to do?" Gloria asked her mother. "If Joey finds out Banjo is dead, he will be heartbroken."

"He's not going to find out," Mary quickly spoke up. "You and I are going to the pet store today to find a replacement that looks just like him."

Gloria chuckled. "You are something, Mom. You always know just what to do."

"Not always," Mary smiled back. "But I do everything I can to keep my children happy."

At that moment, Francine walked up to them holding a little ceramic clock that she had found on the mantle. She smiled, pointed at the clock and muttered something absolutely unintelligible. Gloria just stared blankly at her, but Mary smiled warmly and said, "Funny you should pick that up, Francine. Gloria gave us that clock for our 25th anniversary many years ago. You two must have the same taste!"

Gloria smiled and said, "Of course we do. I married her son, didn't I?!"

Mary chuckled at her daughter's wit, then looked back at Francine and said, "Just be careful with it. Not only is it old, but it is breakable."

Francine smiled as if she understood and wandered off to find something else to explore. Watching her walk away, Gloria said, "I love my mother-in-law, but she can be a real challenge to care for. Sometimes she speaks clearly and I can understand what she is saying. Other times it's just unintelligible garble. And I never get a moment to rest. She's a lot like a toddler, just constantly into everything."

"I know, sweetie," her mother sighed, squeezing her hand. "Elderly people can be more work than children. At least children understand there are some things they can't do and need help with. But the elderly don't want help because they don't want to admit they can't take care of themselves anymore."

Looking at Francine, she sighed and added, "And it's so sad to watch her. She used to be such an intelligent woman."

"Oh, definitely," Gloria agreed, "She knew the stock market like no one I have ever met. She doubled the size of the family estate during her competent years. And now her brain just doesn't work right anymore. But I'll tell you, she retains her arrogance. Sometimes it can be very embarrassing."

Hopping up from the couch, Mary said, "Well, honey, why don't you join me in the kitchen and I will make you a cup of tea. We can chat some more out there."

Gloria stood up to follow her mother, but stopped to look over her shoulder at her mother-in-law, still wandering aimlessly around the living room.

"She's fine," her mother reassured her, taking her by the arm. "She can poke around and explore. We'll just peak in on her every once in awhile to make sure she's okay."

Once in the kitchen, Gloria settled herself onto a stool at her father's new island and her mother put the tea kettle on the freshly cleaned stovetop.

"Nice counter," Gloria commented, rubbing her hands across the smooth countertop.

"Yes, your father is getting quite creative in his retirement," Mary replied. "Look at the spice rack he made, too. Now I can keep my spices organized and find them quickly - without having to empty the cupboard."

Gloria spotted the tray of éclairs and said, "Those look delicious. Did you make them?"

Turning from the stove, Mary looked at the tray of éclairs and said, "Those are Cassandra's creation. She has been learning new skills in her youth group and wanted to demonstrate them for us. We can have some with our tea."

Mary and Gloria were soon lost in conversation, discussing memories of childhood days and talking about events of the twelve day plan. After a time, Francine drifted into the kitchen to see what was happening.

"Hello," Francine said, as she approached the pair chatting at the island. "What a lovely kitchen."

"Well, thank you, Francine," Mary replied, surprised at the clarity of her words. Holding out the tray of éclairs, she asked, "Would you like an éclair?"

Francine carefully inspected the tray filled with delicious-looking éclairs. After a thorough inspection, she finally picked one up gingerly. She held it up and turned it from side-to-side, studying it from every angle.

"These look absolutely delicious," she commented. Looking up at Mary and Gloria, she continued, "But I'm not very hungry right now. I think I will save this for later."

She held out the front pocket of her silky white blouse and gently slid the éclair into it. She licked the chocolate from her fingers, dismissed the two ladies watching her as if they no longer existed, and returned to her exploration of the house.

Picturing the chocolate smearing itself throughout the pocket of her mother-in-law's blouse, Gloria dropped her head onto her father's new countertop. Mary sat and watched Francine walk away, her eyes still wide with surprise and not quite sure what to say next.

"See what I have to put up with?" Gloria asked. "It will probably be easier to just throw the blouse away than to try to get the chocolate stain out."

Mary could see that her daughter was stressed and wanted to help make her day a little easier. It was clear that she needed a break, and decided now would be a good time to go shopping.

"Do you think Jack will be okay with keeping an eye on his mother for awhile?" Mary asked Gloria. "We could take a run to the pet store to find a new little Banjo and just leave Francine to explore around here."

Gloria lifted her head and said, "Oh, Jack is wonderful with his mother. He has more patience with her than I do. I'm sure he wouldn't mind keeping an eye on her."

"Then let's do it," Mary decided.

They went to find the men to present their plan to them. They found them seated in the living room, having a hearty chat. The women proposed their idea of going to the pet store and asked it they could simply keep an eye on Francine. The house was big enough for her to have lots to explore, and they would just need to check on her periodically to make sure she didn't wander off or get into anything she shouldn't. The men agreed and encouraged the ladies to pursue their plan.

Mary headed off to the library and stopped at Banjo's cage.

"What are you doing, Mom?" Gloria asked, following her into the room.

"I will never be able to get another bird to match this one if I don't bring it with me," Mary explained.

Gloria looked quizzically at her mother and asked,

"You're going to bring a dead bird to the pet store with you?"

"How else can I get a bird close enough so that Joey doesn't notice the difference?" Mary questioned, looking up at Gloria to see if she had a better plan.

Gloria shrugged and said, "I guess you can bring it, but you will probably want to keep it hidden in your purse so no one sees it. They might think you are crazy bringing a dead bird to the store with you."

Mary just smiled and said, "I'll just mutter something unintelligible and you can pretend you are my caregiver. Or you can just act like you don't know me."

Gloria smiled and said, "Sad, but I am used to being embarrassed in public by senile old ladies. So it probably won't bother me too much if someone does see you with a dead bird in your pocketbook."

Having finally decided that the bird needed to go with them, Mary set about retrieving him from his cage. There was no way she was going to touch a dead bird with her bare hands. So she headed out to the kitchen and returned a few minutes later with a clear plastic bag and a pair of tongs. With the tongs, she gingerly lifted the bird from the cage and dropped him into the plastic bag.

Gloria wrinkled her nose and said, "That's kind of disgusting, Mom. Maybe we should have let the men deal with the dead bird and we could watch Francine instead."

She paused for a moment as if to ponder the options, then looked at her mother and added, "Forget I said that. Let's go to the pet store."

Mary dropped poor, dead Banjo into her purse and the two ladies made their exit to head to the pet store.

****

Choosing a replacement bird proved to be more of a challenge than either Mary or Gloria had expected. They pointed and compared, and peaked frequently into Mary's purse to check Banjo's markings. What they didn't notice was that Margaret

Wellington, Mary's arch enemy, had made an entrance into the pet store and stood curiously observing their behavior.

Margaret was prone to sticking her nose into other people's business to begin with, but the Davis' ladies behavior seemed quite peculiar. They appeared to be very intent on what they were doing, and completely unaware of anyone around them. Margaret simply couldn't resist the urge to investigate. It didn't appear that they were stealing anything, but if they were, you could believe Pastor Ron would be hearing about it. As she got closer, she could hear the conversation between mother and daughter.

"But no, Mom," Gloria was saying, looking into her mother's purse. "Banjo had a white patch under his chin and that bird doesn't."

"That's true," her mother agreed.

Margaret stealthily moved closer until she was close enough to glance into Mary's open purse. Feeling someone standing nearby, Mary looked up and jumped in surprise.

"Oh, hello, Margaret," she said slowly. "You startled me."

But Margaret didn't return the greeting. Instead, she looked into Mary's purse, then slowly back up at her and asked dryly, "Is that a dead bird in your purse?"

Mary could feel the color creep up her neck and flood her face. She grew angry with herself for letting Margaret Wellington embarrass her like that. Why was that lady always around when she was doing something foolish?

She quickly closed her purse and brushed her hair back, trying to come up with some excuse for why she had a dead bird in her purse. But nothing came to mind, and she had never been good with deceitfulness anyway. So she decided to tell it like it was.

"I'm babysitting for my son's bird, and he died," she explained. Knowing her face was still red and there was nothing she could do about it, she decided to stand her ground and look Margaret right in the eye. When she did, she saw Margaret Wellington looking back at her with a raised eyebrow and a reprimanding look, as if she was about to scold her.

"So you brought his dead bird to the pet store to find another one like it?" Margaret questioned, sounding like Mary's third grade teacher when she got in trouble for the one-and-only time she cheated on a test.

"That pretty much sums it up," Mary smiled nervously.

"Isn't that kind of dishonest?" the pious Mrs. Wellington asked, then quickly added, "Letting your son think it's the same bird instead of telling him the truth?"

Mary was stunned by Margaret's holier-than-thou attitude. Here she was accusing her of being dishonest over a dead bird, when she had stood in front of a whole congregation multiple times and misrepresented the facts to make herself look like a hero. A thousand responses flashed through Mary's overheated brain, but none of them were polite or appropriate, especially in a public place like the pet store at the mall. So instead, she chose a more suitable response.

"Well, I guess, if that's the way you see it," she replied slowly. Then she perked up and bravely added, "But my son is out defending his country right now, and I'm not about to bring his spirits down by telling him his only pet and best friend has died. So if you will excuse us, my daughter and I need to get back to choosing a replacement for him."

And with that, she abruptly turned her back on the pompous Margaret Wellington. In an act of defiance, she reached into her purse, and pulled out the plastic bag containing poor, dead Banjo. Margaret stood there with her mouth gaped open, wearing an expression that ranked somewhere between offended and disgusted. But Mary had already dismissed her and returned to the chore at hand.

"So which one did we choose, Gloria?" she asked her daughter sweetly. Pointing at the dead bird in the bag, she said, "Oh, look how he has this defining ring here. Do you see another one like that?"

Margaret could take no more. She turned in repugnance and stormed out of the pet store.

****

Mary and Gloria laughed all the way home.

"But, Mom, if you could have seen her face!" Gloria laughed.

"I wanted to see her reaction," Mary chuckled, "but I knew I couldn't look at her. I didn't know whether I would laugh or cry - laugh at her reaction or cry because I was thoroughly embarrassed."

She paused, then added, "Who takes a dead bird to the pet store anyway?!!" And both ladies broke into another round of laughter.

The tone of merriment followed them through the front door when they returned to the Davis household. Joseph and Jack were watching football in the living room and looked up in surprise when the giggling ladies rolled through the door. It had been quite some time since Jack had seen Gloria so carefree and happy. He knew caring for his elderly mother was a huge burden for her, and he was glad that she had had a chance to get away from it for a short bout.

"You ladies sound like a couple of frolicking teenagers," Joseph said with a smile.

"I do hope you behaved yourself at the mall," Jack chuckled.

"Oh, Dad," Gloria laughed openly, "You should have seen what Mom just did to Margaret Wellington at the mall!"

Joseph gave Mary a stern look and said, "Mary, what did you do this time?"

Mary shrugged innocently, glanced at Gloria, and both ladies burst into laughter again. They were in the midst of telling their tale about the dead bird in Mary's purse and Margaret's look of horror when Francine wandered into the room. For a brief spell, Gloria had forgotten all about her senile mother-in-law. They paused from their storytelling as Francine bustled over to them. She seemed anxious to tell them something. She walked up to Mary and grinned from ear-to-ear.

"I fixed the Christmas tree while you were out," she said proudly.

Mary thought she had already put everything back into place and wasn't aware that it needed fixing. But Francine seemed so pleased with herself that Mary replied, "Well, thank you, Francine. What exactly did you fix?"

"Oh, just watch this," she said. Acting like a little child about to unwrap the biggest birthday present she had ever received, Francine scooted behind the Christmas tree and plugged it in.

Mary's mouth dropped open in surprise. In their absence, Francine had somehow managed to color code the light bulbs on the Christmas tree. The tree was now layered in colors. All the green bulbs were on the top, followed by layers of yellow, red and blue. It reminded Mary of the toy her children had played with as toddlers, stacking different colored rings orderly on a post.

Realizing Francine was waiting for her reply, she smiled and said, "That's beautiful, Francine. You must have worked very hard on it."

"Oh, yes," said Francine eagerly, "but that's not all I did. Come see this!"

Francine headed for the door to the hallway. Mary followed after her, giving Joseph a look that silently questioned, Where were you when this was taking place?

The four adults followed Francine into the library, where she proudly directed their attention to Joseph's shelves of books. Mary took one look and gasped, covering her mouth with her hand so Francine wouldn't see her surprise. Joseph's books were no longer neatly organized by author. Francine had also color coded the shelves of books that Joseph had spent hours organizing. She had matched binder colors, regardless of shape, size or author.

Mary glanced quickly at Joseph to catch his reaction. The redecorating of the tree didn't matter much. It was only temporary and would be coming down soon anyway. But Joseph had been so proud that he had finally filed his lifetime collection of books by author. And Francine had successfully managed to jumble up his system by categorizing them according to the color of their cover.

Francine seemed totally oblivious to the dubious looks she received from her less than excited audience. They were clearly not as impressed by her work as she was, but she didn't seem to notice at all.

"And one more thing," she said.

"There's more?" Mary asked, looking sideways at Joseph first and then to Gloria.

"Yes, indeed!" smiled Francine proudly. "Right this way!"

She led them into the kitchen, where she proudly pointed out the newly color coded spice rack. Mary had been so happy to have her spices organized and easy to find, but Francine had felt it a better solution to match the color of the labels.

The four reasonable adults stood awkwardly in the kitchen, nobody quite knowing what to say, while Francine giggled with glee and clapped her hands. She was as excited as a kindergartener who had just completed reciting their ABC's correctly for the first time. The fact that there were no jubilant adults to share in her exhilaration was not evident to her.

But it was all too much for Gloria. She dropped onto a stool at the counter, in total defeat, and threw her head into her hands. Seeing how upset Gloria was, Mary looked at Joseph and whispered, "Where were you when she was doing all this?!"

"We were watching football," Joseph whispered back. "She was quiet, so we thought she was okay."

"You should have known better," Mary scolded. "Didn't you help raise twelve kids? And when they got quiet, it always meant they were up to something."

Joseph nodded his head slowly in agreement, pausing to remember how true it was, while Mary walked over to rub Gloria's back. Jack attempted to reason with his mother and reprimand her for tampering with things that didn't belong to her. Mary, the born peace-keeper, reassured everyone that no harm was done. Everything could be put back in its place later.

Thinking that it would do everyone some good to get out of the house, and remembering how successful an event it had been on Noel's day, mom came up with a plan.

"You know, there's a new restaurant in town that I have been wanting to try," she suggested. "Why don't we just go out and get a bite to eat?"

"Good idea," Joseph quickly agreed.

Jack looked at his mother and asked, "But what about my mother? She seems to have something on the front of her blouse."

Gloria looked up quickly in horror. "That's the chocolate éclair she put in her pocket. Is it still in there?"

Jack gingerly reached into the pocket of his mother's white blouse and pulled out a dilapidated chocolate éclair.

"I'm afraid so," he said. "Why did she put a chocolate éclair in her pocket?"

"She wanted to save it for later," Gloria explained, again covering her face with her hands.

Jack studied the front of his mother's blouse for a moment, and then asked, "Well, what should we do? We can't take her out looking like that."

Thinking quickly, Mary volunteered, "Let me just run upstairs and grab a dress coat. She can just wear it over the top of her blouse."

Everyone agreed that would be the easiest solution. Soon they were on their way to the restaurant. In the car, they chatted about how the week had gone so far, and what the plans were for the days still to come.

"Who will be here tomorrow?" Gloria asked.

"That would be your brother, Gary," Mary replied.

"I'm glad you can keep track of it all," Joseph smiled.

"I have it all on my calendar and check it every day," Mary explained. "I would never be able to remember everything if I didn't write it all down."

"How is Gary doing?" Jack questioned. "We haven't

seen much of him since he married and moved to Edson."

"Yeah, we used to spend a lot of time together," sighed Gloria. "Now we pretty much only communicate through the Internet."

"It's not like Edson is that far away," Jack chuckled, "but everyone just seems so busy. It's hard to find the time to get together."

"I know," Mary agreed. "Life is just too fast-paced, and we can't always get together as often as we would like. But Gary calls frequently and keeps in touch. Things seem to be going well for him."

"Does he get along well with Amy's kids?" Gloria asked.

"They seem to be good kids," Joseph offered. "The last time I talked to Gary, he said they seemed to be bonding, and he was enjoying his new role as a dad."

Throughout the trip, Francine sat in the backseat humming and singing to herself. She had been oblivious to the conversation, and didn't even seem to realize she was not alone in the car. But when they pulled into the parking lot at the restaurant, she seemed to come back to life.

"Oh, look at the pretty lights," she exclaimed. "I have always wanted to come here!"

She quickly took her seatbelt off and prepared to jump out of the car. Gloria looked questioningly at Jack, who just shrugged his shoulders in reply. Their silent conversation said, *Did she really want to come here, or is she just having another delusional episode?* Either way, it didn't really matter. Francine had almost made it to the entrance of the restaurant and they would need to hustle to catch up with her.

The interior of the restaurant was set up in Western style. The chandeliers were made of antlers. Saddles hung across the rafters, and the floor was covered with peanut shells. As the hostess led them to their table, the Davis family soon discovered why. As patrons ate peanuts for their appetizer, they discarded the empty shells on the floor.

"I would hate to have to clean these floors," Gloria whispered softly to her mother, as she walked gingerly across the scattered peanut shells.

"It is a bit of a mess," her mother agreed.

The hostess seated the party of five and everyone placed their orders. Mary sat back and smiled smugly. It appeared they had managed to save the day. Gloria seemed to be enjoying herself and was much more relaxed than she had been back at the house. Francine seemed preoccupied with checking out the condiments located in the middle of the table, and was currently being quiet and well-behaved.

But then the waitress set a bowl of peanuts in the middle of the table for them to snack on while they waited for their dinner, and that's all it took to upset the apple cart.

"Oh, I see," commented Joseph. "You just throw your peanut shells on the floor when you are done."

"Aw, mystery solved," Jack agreed. "I thought it was unusual to have so many shells on the floor."

Mary and Gloria smiled at each other, having solved the mystery sometime ago. But they wouldn't burst the men's bubbles. They seemed happy to have figured it out on their own.

Everyone grabbed a peanut and started to crack it open. Everyone except Francine, that is. She grabbed a peanut and, before anyone could stop her, popped the whole thing in her mouth, shell and all.

"Oh, no," exclaimed Gloria, worried that her mother-in-law would choke.

"No, Mom," Jack said, quickly jumping up and coming to her assistance. "They are unshelled peanuts. You have to take the shell off first."

Francine quickly realized the error, but not as her mistake. She was horrified that the restaurant would serve unshelled peanuts, and she was going to let them know about it. Her residue of arrogance kicked in, and she flagged down the first waiter she could find.

"You there!" she demanded, calling loudly across the restaurant with an accusing finger pointed at the innocent boy. "What is the meaning of this?!"

The unsuspecting waiter came over to see how he could be of assistance, but then stood open-mouthed and red faced as she continued her tyrant.

"Why would any restaurant serve peanuts that are not shelled?" Francine demanded. "I could have choked on these. You better believe my lawyer will be calling."

"I'm sorry, ma'am," the young waiter started. "But that is part of our style. We are a 'Western style' restaurant, so we serve foods like the old west. Cowboys didn't buy their peanuts in a bag already shelled."

"Are you trying to mock me?" Francine railed. "Do you think this is a joke?"

The waiter's face only grew redder. And Gloria's face only grew longer. She was ready to crawl under the table.

"I would like to speak to your manager, young man," Francine shouted, standing up and drawing the attention of all the tables surrounding them.

That was all Gloria could take. She burst into tears and hid her face behind her hands. Jack jumped up to grab his mother, trying to encourage her to sit down.

"It's okay, Mom," he insisted. "Just please quiet down. Have a seat and let's talk about this while we wait for our food."

"Food!" shouted Francine. "I wouldn't eat here if it was the last place on earth. Where is the manager?!!"

"I'll go get him, ma'am," the red-faced waiter said, anxious to flee the scene.

"No, no, you don't need to," Jack assured him. "My mother just needs to settle down. Everything is fine."

Mary felt totally helpless. She had successfully rescued the last couple of days when a crisis had erupted, but she had met her match with Francine. All she could do was put an arm around Gloria, rub her shoulder, and reassure her that everything would be okay.

Trying to look on the bright side, Mary told her daughter, "You know, sweetie, someday you are going to look back at this and laugh about it. The other day, Luke and I were talking about how the things that upset you the most always make the funniest memories.”

“If that is true,” Gloria reasoned between sobs, “then someday this will be a hysterical memory!”

****

****

Garland

****

Chapter 7
Garland

★★★★★★★

Day Six arrived and Mary was still in good spirits. They had hit a few snags during the last few days, but most of her children had left happy. Except for poor Gloria. The two of them had shared some laughs, and put the self-righteous Margaret Wellington in her place, so it hadn't been a total loss.

Mom had changed the decoration on the front door, wrapping a string of garland around Gary's sign. They rarely called him Garland, but occasionally she liked to remind him of his legal name. Today would be the first time they had spent quality time together with Gary's new family, and Mary was looking forward to getting to know his stepsons a little better.

Gary had only recently married Amy. It was a package deal that came with two tweens. Ethan was twelve and Brody was two years younger. Gary had never had children of his own, but had jumped into the role of father eagerly. Yet, never having had biological children left Gary at a bit of a disadvantage. He had missed the baby stage, skipped over the early childhood years and landed squarely in the middle of the preteen days. But he was confident that he could handle the challenge.

Mary had big plans for their day together. Having two active boys coming, she had decided a day at the sledding park would keep them occupied, but would prove fun for the whole family. She had gone to the store and purchased snow tubes for the day's event. While she waited for Gary's family to arrive, she busied herself with finding boots, hats, and gloves to wear.

It had been a long time since she had been sledding, and tubing would be a new adventure for both her and

Grandpa Joseph. This was going to be an enjoyable day, and Mary could hardly contain her excitement while waiting for her company to arrive. She wanted to make a good impression on her new grandsons, and an activity like this was sure to aid in the bonding process.

"I'm going to get the mail," Joseph announced, stopping to watch Mary for a moment. Her head was completely out of sight as she bent over the basket in the hallway closet, digging for winter clothing. For a moment, he thought she hadn't heard him. But then she stood up and turned to face him, with hair all askew and cheeks red from her inadvertent posture.

"Cute 'do," he smiled, "but you might want to get your hair under control before Amy and the boys get here. You don't want to scare them away."

"Ha, ha," Mary said, turning back to the mess she had made in the closet. "I just can't seem to find a pair of matching gloves."

"Don't worry about it," Joseph said, putting his coat on. "Kids don't match their socks anymore. Maybe you'll start a trend of mismatched gloves."

Mary mumbled something from the closet, and Joseph just chuckled as he walked out the door. He probably didn't want to know what she had said anyway.

As Joseph exited the house, he saw Sam, the mailman. Sam had just put mail in the Davis mailbox at the end of the walkway. Looking Joseph's way, he called, "Morning, Joseph."

"Morning, Sam," Joseph called back.

As Sam turned to continue his route, Joseph noticed that Buzzy was nipping at his heels.

"I see you have your daily help, as usual," Joseph commented.

Looking down at the obnoxious dog, Sam said, "One would think he would get tired of it after awhile. I know I'm tired of buying new boots all the time. The heels seem to wear out rather quickly!"

Joseph chuckled and said, "I don't know how you do it,

Sam. I'm afraid I wouldn't be that patient. I would either end up kicking him in the butt or smacking him across the head to knock some sense into him."

Sam just smiled and said, "Have a good day!"

Joseph waved and went to retrieve his mail. As he turned to head back into the house, Gary and his family drove into the yard.

By the time the family had unloaded from the car and made it into the house, Mary had found everything they needed for a day filled with outdoor wintertime fun. She had shared her plans with Gary, and he had agreed it sounded like something the boys would enjoy. So they had come prepared, complete with hats, mittens, boots and winter apparel.

After hugs and kisses, Mary asked, "So, where should we begin? Do you want to go sledding first and then come home to warm up with a cup of hot cocoa?"

Everyone agreed that was a good plan, so they set about donning their outdoor apparel to prepare for the chilly winter weather.

"I bought some new snow tubes," Mary announced. "They looked like fun and our sleds have long since gone away, probably sold in a yard sale some time ago."

"They were outdated anyway," Joseph added.

Gary chuckled. "Yeah, those old wooden runner sleds were fun, but not very practical."

"It's a wonder more kids didn't get hurt with them," Amy agreed, remembering her youthful sledding excursions.

"Whatever happened to that big old toboggan we used to have?" Gary asked.

"You know, we might still have that," Grandma Mary smiled.

"I think I saw it hanging on the wall in the garage when I was looking for my net the other day," Grandpa Joseph stated. "The garage is a project I haven't taken on yet, but I might be able to get the toboggan off the wall. Do you want me to try?"

Gary smiled and said, "If it's not too much work. It would be fun to take it for another spin down the hill."

Grandpa Joseph went to assess the situation to determine if the toboggan would be able to join them for the day. In his absence, the rest of the family continued their preparations and chatted about their plans for the day.

"I want to use the tubes," Brody stated.

"Yeah! Tubing is a lot of fun," agreed big brother, Ethan. "You old folks can use the toboggan."

Amy glanced at Gary, not sure if Ethan's comment needed to be followed by a reprimand. He just smiled and winked at her. No sense in getting off to a rough start. They would just let it go this time.

"That's fine with me," Grandma Mary said, finally conquering the task of getting her stubborn boot on. "I only bought two tubes anyway, so you boys can use the tubes and we will use the toboggan, if Grandpa Joseph can find it."

Grandpa Joseph came back just then stating he had located the toboggan, and was actually able to retrieve it. It was a bit dusty, but still in good shape. Maybe if they swept it off a bit, they could wash the rest of the dust off with good, old-fashioned snow. Before he could finish his statement, Brody let out with a growl.

Everyone looked up, startled. At first Grandma Mary thought he was upset that the toboggan was dirty or that she had only bought two snow tubes. Buying more tubes didn't make sense for just one day of entertainment. Grandma Mary and Grandpa Joseph certainly didn't plan on using them again.

However, it quickly became clear that he was not upset about either the snow tubes or the toboggan. Before anyone could ask what the problem was, his winter boot came sailing across the room, narrowly missing his brother's head. Gary tried to grab it as it flew past him, but proved unsuccessful. Everyone watched in horror as the boot made direct contact with Grandma Mary's special vase from Vienna, sending it crashing to the floor.

"My vase!" Grandma Mary gasped, dropping down onto the couch in a state of shock.

There was a long moment of stunned silence, with nobody quite sure what to do or say. Horror and alarm were the expressions written on each face. The adults knew how much that vase meant to Grandma Mary. And the kids didn't know Grandma Mary well enough to know what was coming next. Was she going to kick them out and tell them to go home? Cancel their fun day of sledding? Tell them they were never welcome there again? Throw something back at Brody?

Then Amy broke the silence. "Brody!" she called out in disbelief and alarm. "Look what you did to Grandma Mary's vase!"

Grandma Mary's face took on a mixture of emotions. She was devastated that her beautiful hand-painted vase which she had painstakingly brought home from Vienna now lay in pieces on her living room floor. She was worried that this day was ruined before it even got started. And she was totally baffled as to what brought the outburst of anger to begin with.

Grandpa Joseph and Grandma Mary quickly set about cleaning up the pieces of the vase. They carried them out to the kitchen and left Gary and Amy to deal with the distraught Brody.

Looking at the pieces laying on the counter, Mary was close to tears.

"First my cuckoo clock, and now my vase from Vienna," she moaned.

"I might be able to piece this back together," Joseph tried to reassure her. "It's amazing what a little Super Glue can do."

He gave Mary a supportive hug and added, "Once the holidays are over and things settle down, I'll try to fix both the clock and the vase."

Gary and Amy came into the kitchen just then with a less than happy Brody. His head hung low and he looked close to tears.

"Brody has something he wants to say to you," Gary

announced.

Brody just stood there, looking completely dejected, and about as sad as a boy could be.

"Brody?" his mother said, encouraging him to speak.

"I'm very sorry, Grandma Mary," he stumbled. "I know that vase was very special to you, and I'm sorry I broke it."

Seeing he was close to tears, Grandma Mary rushed over to give him a hug. "I know you didn't do it on purpose," she reassured him. "Accidents happen."

Ethan joined them just then and said, "Brody's going to save his allowance and try to repay you."

"Oh, that's not necessary," Grandma Mary stated. "I can't replace the vase anyway."

Brody's head came up sharply and it looked like there was no stopping the flow of tears that were ready to unleash at any moment. Realizing what she had just said hadn't helped the situation, Grandma Mary quickly added, "I mean, it's not like we'll be going to Europe again anytime soon." Realizing she was only digging a deeper ditch for herself, she changed the topic. "Let's go tubing. Is everyone ready?"

They all decided it was time to get out of the house, forget the recent trauma, and move onto some good old-fashioned family fun. So they finished dressing for the weather and went to load up the car.

As Joseph contemplated how to fit the tubes into the car, Gary came to stand beside his mother, putting an arm around her shoulder.

"Are you okay?" he asked, looking at her with a concerned expression.

"I'm fine, sweetie," his mother reassured him, giving him a quick hug and resting her head against his shoulder.

"It's just that I know how excited you were about that vase and how hard you worked to get it home in one piece - only to have my distraught son destroy it with a flying boot in your own living room," Gary sympathized.

Mary smiled and squeezed her son's arm. "It's only a materialistic item. I will find another one like it somewhere,

I'm sure."

"But it won't be the same," Gary stated. He paused, and then added, "So, as you can see, Brody has some anger issues. He was upset that he couldn't get his boot on. He's been through a lot, with his dad leaving them and his mom remarrying. It's all been traumatic for him, but we have him in counseling, and hopefully he will come around."

"He'll be fine, honey," Mary reassured her son, "especially with a loving, supportive father like you."

"Thanks for your vote of confidence, Mom," Gary said, giving his mother a kiss on the forehead. Then as they watched Grandpa Joseph struggling with the snow tubes, he added, "Right now, I think we need to go rescue Grandpa Joseph!"

It was clear that Grandpa Joseph was not having fun. As hard as he tried, he just couldn't seem to get both snow tubes to fit in the backseat of the car. He had successfully gotten the first tube in, but the second one just wouldn't cooperate. In frustration, he walked around the car and opened the door on the other side, only to be greeted by the first tube rolling out and landing at his feet.

"Okay, Grandpa," said Gary, coming to his father's rescue. "I have an idea. Let's just take two separate vehicles. We'll put a boy and a tube in the backseat of each car."

"Sounds like a plan to me," agreed an exasperated Joseph. "And we'll strap the toboggan on the roof rack."

"Can I ride with you?" Brody asked, looking up at Grandma Mary shyly.

Grandma Mary looked from Brody to Gary with a surprised expression, then quickly recovered and said, "Why sure you can, sweetie! Grandpa Joseph and I would love to have you ride with us."

So with the seating arrangements determined, they loaded up the cars and headed for the town recreational area to do some sledding. Brody proved to be a talkative, entertaining child. He was animated in his conversation, telling about previous sledding experiences and how his brother sent him over "The Bump" at home. At first, he claimed it was fun, but then admitted that it did kind of hurt when he landed.

Grandma Mary asked if he ever went ice skating. He said he didn't have much luck with ice skates. He had always wanted to play ice hockey, but he couldn't seem to stand up with skates on. He spent most of his time down on the ice. Grandpa Joseph and Grandma Mary enjoyed the conversation and chuckled at his energetic talk.

****

It didn't take long to get to the park, and soon everyone was out of the car and heading to the hill to do some sledding. The boys outran the adults, carrying the tubes with them, while Gary trudged along behind them pulling the dusty, old toboggan.

Watching them run ahead of her, Grandma Mary said, "I should have bought more tubes," suddenly realizing that two tubes for six people was relatively inadequate.

"Oh, that's fine," Amy reassured her. "This is more of an outing for the boys anyway. We are getting too old for climbing up and down the hillside. They will probably enjoy the activity more than we will! I'm good with remaining stationary and just watching."

"Yeah, let them do all the work," Gary chuckled, and then added, "but if you really want to go sledding, I'm sure the boys will share a tube with you. Or you can take a run on the toboggan."

Grandpa Joseph smiled and said, "I agree with Amy. Observation and staying put sound good to me."

Grandpa Joseph's back still hadn't quite recovered from his fall off the ladder. The snowman had deflated so fast that he had hit the ground a little harder than he had wanted, not that he had wanted to hit the ground at all!

Grandma Mary just smiled and nodded, watching the boys sail off down the hill. They quickly jumped off the tubes at the bottom and climbed back up to join the cluster of adults still making their way painstakingly to the top.

"Whew," said Grandpa Joseph, pausing at the top to catch his breath. "I thought I was in better shape than this."

"Wow, me too," Grandma Mary agreed. "Running on the treadmill just isn't the same as climbing uphill."

"Who wants to go now?" Brody asked, looking from one adult to another.

The adults, however, were still winded and had already agreed that observing would be more fun. It wasn't the trip down they were concerned about. It was the climb back up. Once might just be enough.

"You guys go ahead," Gary encouraged them.

"I'll race you," Ethan said to his younger brother, jumping on his tube.

The boys whirled and twirled their way down the hill. The adults watched from their perch at the top, laughing as the pair whizzed down to the base. It was a close race at first, but then Ethan quickly passed by Brody. Being two years his senior gave him the advantage of being bigger and heavier. With more momentum, beating Brody to the bottom was not difficult. Brody didn't appear to be discouraged, though. He seemed to have accepted the fact that his older brother was bigger, stronger, and frequently outdid him.

Watching them retrieve their tubes and make their way back up to the top of the hill, Amy said, "This was such a good idea."

"That's my mom," Gary explained, "just one good idea after another."

Mary smiled and patted her son on the back. "With twelve kids to keep up with, I had to be thinking and planning all the time."

The four adults turned their attention to the two boys frolicking in the winter snow and gradually making their way back up the hill. Ethan playfully threw a handful of snow at his younger brother, who just as playfully threw one back. Mary smiled and thought to herself, *What nice boys they are. Gary is going to be a wonderful father for them.*

Upon reaching the waiting adults, the boys didn't waste any time in taking another spin down the hillside. But by the third time of climbing back to the top, they were ready for a break.

"Grandma Mary, why don't you try the tube out?" Brody suggested.

"Yeah," Ethan agreed, "you bought them, so you ought to give them a whirl."

"Oh, I don't know," said Mary, hesitantly. "I haven't been sledding for years. I think I'm too old for it."

"Nonsense," said Gary, deciding maybe a spin down the hillside might be fun after all. "You're never too old to go sledding. Come on, I'll race you."

He grabbed a tube and sat down, ready to take a downhill flight. The two boys held the other tube for Grandma Mary as she slowly and hesitantly climbed onboard.

When mother and son were seated and ready to go, Amy stepped between the tubes and gave the starting command. "On your mark, get set - Go!"

As they pushed Grandma Mary off, Ethan and Brody gave her a bit of a twist. She swirled and twirled down the hillside, spinning from top to bottom. Gary, having the weight advantage, quickly passed her by to win the race. When gram slid to a stop at the foot of the hill, she was so dizzy from spinning that she could hardly even stand up. Gary quickly rushed to her aid, steadying her as she regained her balance.

"Wow, am I ever dizzy!" she exclaimed. She struggled to take a step or two and said, "I don't know if I will ever be able to walk right again."

She dropped back down on her tube to rest, and Gary couldn't help but chuckle. When she was ready to try again, Gary helped her struggle to her feet. Together, the two of them laughed and chatted as they worked their way back up the hill.

When they finally reached the group waiting for them at the top, Ethan immediately grabbed a tube and said, "Now it is Grandpa Joseph's turn."

Grandpa Joseph laughed and said, "Oh, no, I don't think so."

Grandma Mary smiled and said, "Oh, I do! If I can go tubing, you can, too."

There was a chorus of agreement that Grandpa Joseph should indeed try the tubing experience.

"Okay, okay, I will," he finally agreed. "But not until everyone else has had a turn, and not until we are ready to leave. I want to be the last run of the day, just incase my back gives out. I don't want to ruin the outing."

"Okay, fair enough," Gary said. "Just don't back out on us."

"It's the 'back' part that I'm worried about," Joseph said, laughing at his own humor.

After reassuring them he would keep his part of the bargain, the group redirected their attention to the snow-covered hill. The boys wanted to make sure everyone had ample opportunities to utilize the tubes. The adults, of course, allowed the boys to have the greatest number of turns. But they did work in a few runs for Gary and Amy, and even one more for Grandma Mary. No one seemed interested in riding the toboggan, but it proved to be a good seat for those left behind at the top of the hill.

During their trips down the hillside, Ethan and Brody had discovered a huge jump. So far no one had managed to sail over it, but in their climb time between slides, they decided to save that bump for Grandpa Joseph's last ride. On their final climb to the top, the boys visually scoped out the bump and plotted Grandpa's path of descent.

"Oh, man," said Ethan, in awe of the massive bump. "That looks like the 'bump of death!'"

"Yeah, the 'bump of death,'" Brody echoed.

Ethan smiled to himself and said, "If Grandpa Joseph hits that bump right, he probably won't touch down again until he reaches the next county!"

"Yeah," Brody said, anxious to agree with anything his brother said, even if he didn't always understand what he meant.

"We gotta do it," Ethan said eagerly. "We gotta give Grandpa Joe the ride of his life. He will never forget it!"

"Yeah," Brody blindly agreed. "We gotta do it!"

When they finally reached the top of the hill, the boys announced that they had had enough tubing. It was now time for Grandpa Joseph's ride down the mountain.

Grandpa Joseph, staying true to his word, climbed onto the tube and prepared to make his descent. What he didn't realize was that his conniving grandsons had lined him up with the massive "bump of death." He had no idea that he was about to encounter a trip that he would never forget! The boys anxiously gave him a push to send him on his way, and then could hardly contain themselves as they waited to see if their plan would work.

"Go, Grandpa Joe!" Brody shouted, bouncing up and down.

"Yeah, go, old man, go!" Ethan chuckled to himself.

Amy looked at her eldest son and asked, "That wasn't meant to be derogative, was it?"

"No," stated Ethan. "I'm just telling it like it is. He is a man, and he is old."

Amy and Gary looked at each other, and then back at Ethan. They weren't quite sure what to do, but Mary put their minds to rest.

"It's okay," she insisted, "Ethan is right. He is a man, and he is getting old. Older than yesterday, anyway!"

They all chuckled to ease the tension and turned their attention back to Grandpa Joseph's plight. Just as they did, he hit the "bump of death." He and his tube left the ground and went air born, for what seemed to Grandma Mary to be just short of forever. She gasped and covered her mouth with her hand. Then moving her hands over her eyes, she said, "I can't watch!"

Gary and Amy watched for her, unable to take their eyes off Grandpa Joseph, for fear of where he might end up. Not that they could do anything to help him anyway. Behind them, Ethan and Brody roared with laughter.

"Look at him go!" shouted Brody.

"What a wild ride," chuckled Ethan.

Right about then, Grandpa Joseph would have been in complete agreement with the boys. This was about the wildest ride he had ever been on. The problem was that it was about to come to a crashing end, and he was powerless to stop it.

The gang at the top had decided they needed to get to the bottom of the hill as soon as possible. Wherever Grandpa Joseph landed, he was probably going to need their help getting up.

"I'll try to catch up with him," Gary said, grabbing the remaining tube and flying off down the hillside.

The remaining four turned the toboggan around and hopped onto it. Their problem was that in the haste to go help her husband, Grandma Mary had inadvertently placed herself in the front, not realizing this gave her the role of steering the toboggan. It soon became apparent that she had no idea how to steer as they began a reckless ride, careening crazily down the hillside and abruptly landing in the brush off the side of the trail.

Meanwhile, Grandpa Joseph could see the ground quickly rising up to meet him and knew his flight was about to end. As the ground got closer, he braced himself, since there wasn't a thing he could do to avoid the fall. This was going to hurt, and it was probably going to hurt bad!

The crash came all too quickly, and pain jolted through his body. Even though he was now on the ground, the tube had gained such speed that it was not at all interested in coming to a rest. It seemed to have a mind of its own, and it wasn't stopping until the game was over.

Grandpa Joseph sailed straight across the landing at the foot of the hill and up the snow pile on the other side. Unfortunately, there was a skating rink located on the opposite side of the snow pile. It was quite crowded with late morning skaters, and Grandpa's snow tube was still out-of-control.

Clearing the top of the snow pile, the tube again took on air. He flew like a chickadee being chased by a vulture, wildly and with no goal in mind other than to survive.

Grandpa once again crashed down to earth and slid uncontrollably across the slippery surface of the ice. As he did, he knocked down innocent skaters, leaving them to fall like Dominoes. In fact, if he were bowling, he would probably have just scored a strike. Young and old, the skaters fell left and right as Grandpa Joseph plowed right through the middle of them.

The tube finally exhausted its energy and came to rest on the far side of the rink. Grandpa Joseph's body was wracked with pain from the rough, out-of-control ride, but he was more concerned about the skaters he had just knocked over. He climbed off his tube and tried to rush to their rescue.

However, instead of being a hero and coming to right the wrong he had caused, he only proved to make the situation worse. The ice was so slippery that when he tried to help a skater up, both parties lost their footing and fell again. He apologized profusely, but was unable to upright any of the fallen skaters after several attempts.

Just then, a booming voice came over the speaker saying, "Old man, get off the ice before you hurt someone."

Grandpa Joseph looked at the announcer's booth, from where the voice had come, and said, "I'm sorry. I was just trying to help."

Instead of thanking him for his effort and asking if he was okay, the voice simply replied, "And take your tube with you. No sledding apparatus is allowed on the ice."

Before Grandpa Joseph could think of a reply, Gary came running over to meet him.

"Are you okay, Dad?" he asked anxiously.

"Can't tell for sure," Grandpa Joseph replied. "I'm sure it's not going to feel good tomorrow, but I'm still able to move right now."

Gary grabbed the tube and escorted his father off the slippery ice. Grandpa Joseph was unable to stand up straight, but remained more concerned about the damage he had caused. As they made their way across the rink, he again apologized to the fallen skaters. Some were making efforts to get back on their feet, while others just sat and glared at him, as if waiting for him to leave before they resumed their upright positions.

Shuffling across the ice like a penguin, Grandpa Joseph kept trying to make amends.

"I'm so sorry," he said to one little girl. To another, he asked, "Are you okay?" Turning to another downed skater, he said, "My apologies."

Some skaters reassured him that they were okay and not upset with the mishap, while others seemed frozen in time, simply watching him make his way off the ice. Gary helped his father back to the remainder of the group, who looked like they had had an adventure of their own. Grandma Mary's hat was on crooked and she had twigs in her hair. And they were all covered with an excessive amount of snow.

"Are you okay, Joseph?" Mary anxiously asked, rushing to the aid of her crippled husband.

"Just ducky!" he replied, putting his hand on his aching back. Looking at her, he asked "And what happened to you?"

She righted her hat and tried to smooth out her hair. "I discovered I don't know how to steer a toboggan," she explained. "That's why it took us awhile to get here. I drove us off the trail, and we all landed in the brush on the side of the trail."

Pausing, she added, "All those years the kids rode that toboggan, and no one ever told me that the person in the front needs to steer!"

Even in as much pain as he was, Grandpa Joseph had to chuckle at his wife's antics. He could just picture them flying off the trail and landing in the brush. Thank goodness there weren't any trees for them to crash into. Things might not have ended quite as well.

"Why don't we go back to the house and chill out," Gary suggested.

"Good idea," Amy agreed. "I'll help Grandma Mary make some hot chocolate so we can all warm up."

Turning to address her offspring, Grandma Mary added, "And you can 'chill' if you want to, but I'm ready for something hot to drink!"

Gary smiled at his mother and the group set their focus on heading for the parked cars. Ethan and Brody led the way, pulling the tubes behind them and chatting excitedly about what a fun time they had had.

"Did you see Grandpa Joe go?" asked Ethan.

"Yeah, that was awesome," agreed Brody.

Next in the line up came Gary and Amy.

"Wow, I'm not as young as I used to be," Amy said, rubbing a sore spot in her back.

"Yeah," agreed Gary, "I think I might feel this tomorrow morning when I try to get out of bed."

Bringing up the rear was Grandma Mary, fussing over her hobbling husband.

"Are you sure you're okay, honey?" she asked him. "Do you want to ride on the toboggan. I can't steer it, but I'm sure I could pull you on it if you hurt too much to walk."

"No, no," he reassured her. "I'll be fine once I'm home and in my recliner."

****

When they got back to the house, they settled Grandpa Joseph into his easy chair and made him a cup of coffee. Grandma Mary, Amy, and the boys had hot chocolate while Gary joined his father in the living room with a cup of coffee of his own. After finishing their hot chocolate, the boys went to play video games in the library and the ladies started working on lunch.

"I hope Grandpa Joe is okay," Amy said.

"I hope so, too," said Mary, optimistically. "At least tomorrow is Sunday, so he can rest." Looking at Amy, she smiled and added, "After all, Sunday is supposed to be a day of rest, right?!"

Amy smiled at her mother-in-law's humor and said, "So speaking of tomorrow, who is coming next?"

"It's Candy's turn," Mary said. "Her husband wasn't able to take the day off, so she will be coming alone with the kids. He has his own church to manage, you know, and there wasn't anyone available to cover for him."

"That's too bad he won't be able to join you," Amy said.

"I know," Mary agreed, "but it's not like they live so far away that we can't go visit them. And Joshua has a birthday coming up in January, so we will probably get to spend time with them then."

"Oh," Amy said suddenly. "I almost forgot."

She paused from the task of making sandwiches and went to find her purse. She came back a few minutes later carrying a pair of tongs. "Gloria called us last night," she explained. "She told us you needed a new pair of tongs."

Mary had to laugh. At least Gloria still had a sense of humor. Now she could throw out the tongs she had used on Joey's dead bird, and do it quickly before she forgot and accidentally used them again. After the holidays, she would be sure to send her a "Thank you" card!

****

****

Candy

****

Chapter 8
Candy

☆☆☆☆☆☆☆

It had been a full week of entertaining guests, and Mary was starting to feel a bit fatigued. Plus, the sledding excursion had left her body aching all over. She had faired the storm better than Joseph, though. Poor Joseph could hardly make his way out of bed this morning. His ride over the "bump of death" had left him with a back of pain. He had decided to forego today's activities and spend the day resting in his recliner.

Mary had helped to settle him into his easy chair and then had hurried to change the scene on her front door to candy canes. Now she was anxiously awaiting the arrival of her seventh child, along with her three offspring.

Joshua was the oldest of the three children. He was seven years old, soon to be eight. His brother, Benjamin, was two years his junior. Little Hannah was three years old, and as cute as they come. Candy had been so happy when God had blessed her with a daughter. She loved her boys, of course, but she had always wanted a little girl to dress up and show off.

Since it was a Sunday, Mary and Candy had decided to go to church together. Candy was looking forward to attending her childhood church and seeing some of her old acquaintances. Even though she didn't live far away, she rarely had the opportunity to go to church with her parents as her husband led a church of his own. So today she came with excitement and high hopes.

Candy arrived on Day Seven and smiled at the thoughtfully placed candy canes on the front door. Then she opened the door quickly before her restless boys charged through it. She held Hannah on her hip, still finding it easier to carry her than to take the time of letting her walk on her own.

After the greetings, Candy stifled a sigh of disappointment, realizing that her father would not be joining them. But after hearing of his sledding excursion, she could sympathize and be thankful for the fact that he could still move at all. She knew how he had struggled with back problems for most of his life. Plus, she was familiar with the "bump of death" at the local recreational area. That bump could weaken even a healthy back!

Grandpa Joseph looked proudly at his grandchildren. "Don't you boys look handsome, all dressed up for church," he complimented them. They beamed and went to give their grandfather a hug.

"Sorry you can't come with us, Grandpa," Joshua said.

"Yeah," Benjamin added, "we're gonna miss you."

Grandpa Joseph just chuckled. "You'll have so much fun in Children's Church, you won't even think about me."

He turned his attention to little Hannah, and said, "Don't you look pretty with a bow in you hair and such a beautiful dress."

"Oh yes," said Candy, "and don't forget about the bow on the back of the dress. She hasn't wanted to take this dress off since Grandma Mary gave it to her. I almost need to bribe her to take it off long enough to wash it."

Grandma Mary smiled and said, "Well, I don't blame her. She looks absolutely beautiful in it."

She paused for a moment, and then added, "But we better get going so we aren't late for church."

Candy kissed her father on the forehead and said, "We will miss having you with us today, Dad. I know you would rather be with us than in agony in that chair. But we will say a prayer for you."

"Thank you, sweetie," he said, smiling up at her. "Maybe I'll be feeling better when you get back and we can do something fun together."

Mary kissed her husband good-bye and told him they would be home as soon as they could. Then she and Candy loaded the kids into the car and headed for the Enfield

Congregational Church. Today they would be in the house of God, a peaceful place to gather. What could possibly go wrong in a setting like that?

****

Candy was surprised when Pastor Ron met them at the church door. He was the minister that had performed her wedding ceremony close to a decade ago, and she hadn't seen him for years.

"Candy!" he said, immediately recognizing her. "It's so good to see you. How have you been?"

"Just fine, Pastor Ron," she replied. "It's good to see you, too."

Looking at her three children, he said, "I see you have been busy."

"Oh, yes," said Mary quickly, noticing the subtle shade of red appearing on her daughter's cheeks. "Her children keep her very busy."

Candy introduced her children to Pastor Ron. He was glad to have new children join them and told them they would have fun in Children's Church with Miss Lighthart.

"Is she still teaching?" Candy asked, astonished. Looking at her children, she explained, "She was my Sunday School teacher when I was your age!"

Candy and her mother escorted the two boys down to Children's Church, and then headed back upstairs to find a seat in the sanctuary. Mary and Candy had decided to keep Hannah with them during the service as opposed to leaving her in a nursery room full of strangers. Plus, Candy was confident that she would sit quietly. After all, they practically lived in a church, so Hannah was used to the routine.

The boys, on the other hand, were a different story. As hard as Candy had tried, she could not get them to sit still or remain quiet. Maybe it was just because they were boys, and sitting still wasn't part of their nature. But for today, anyway, they would have more fun in Children's Church where they could actively participate and do creative activities.

****

Miss Lighthart was excited to see extra children in her classroom. Her philosophy had always followed "The more, the merrier" train of thought. Today they would be talking about the birth of Jesus, and it was her favorite story in the entire Bible. The more people she could share the story with, the greater her contribution to the world. This was the most important story in all of history, and here were two new souls to share it with.

After getting the children settled down and introducing herself, she anxiously dove into the lesson time.

"Okay, children," she began, "today we are going to talk about the greatest story ever told. Do you know what that story might be?"

She paused to wait for a response from the children, and an excited little girl raised her hand. Miss Lighthart pointed to her, always pleased to have involvement from the children. She felt they learned more when they were actively involved in the conversation.

The little girl quickly spoke up, announcing her mother reads bedtime stories to her every night.

"My mom reads nursery rhymes to me," another child offered. "My favorite is 'Hickory, Dickory, Dock.'"

Another little boy anxiously joined the conversation and added, "I know that one. 'The mouse ran up the clock.'"

"Yuck," a little girl named Emma shuddered. "I hate mice!"

"Mice are cool," Joshua stated. As the oldest child in the classroom, he felt the need to prove how big and brave he was.

"Yeah," Benjamin said, stepping into the conversation. "We used to have a pet mouse. His name was Buddy."

Benjamin paused a moment to reflect on his relationship

with Buddy, then took on a sad expression.

"But Buddy committed…," he paused, not sure of what he was trying to say. He turned to look at his older brother and asked, "What was that second word, Josh?"

"Suicide," Joshua stated, matter-of-factly. "Mom said he committed suicide because he jumped into the toilet and died."

"That's right!" Benjamin smiled, proud that they had remembered the correct terminology. "He committed suicide."

Miss Lighthart gasped, realizing the topic had taken a turn she wished to avoid. She didn't want the children to return to their parents and tell them their today's lesson had covered topics like mice or committing suicide! And this had nothing to do with the greatest story of all time, which is what they were supposed to be talking about.

She clapped her hands to get their attention, and said, "Okay, children. Let's talk about the Bible stories so I can tell you about the best one of all."

Miss Lighthart gently explained that the Bible has lots of good stories, like Jonah and the Whale, Noah's Ark, and Joseph with his coat of many colors. But the greatest story was about Jesus, who had a miraculous birth.

"What does that mean?" one little girl asked curiously.

"It means his birth was a miracle," Miss Lighthart patiently explained. "Do you know what a miracle is?"

"Oh, I think I know," Benjamin said, thoughtfully. "I think it's like when you're in a desert and you see things that aren't really there."

"That's a mirage," Miss Lighthart explained. "You're right, you do see things that are not really there. But it's not a miracle, like the miracle it took to make Jesus."

"How come it took a miracle to make Jesus?" little Emma asked.

"Because His father was God," Miss Lighthart explained, with a smile on her face.

"My mom said God is my father, too," Benjamin said, nodding his head up and down. "Does that mean I'm a miracle, too, just like Jesus?"

Miss Lighthart smiled gently, as she looked around at the innocent little faces in her classroom. Children were so basic and tenderhearted. No wonder they held such a special place in her heart. And this new little soul in her class today seemed so interested in hearing the gospel.

"Well, yes, sweetie," she smiled at Benjamin. "You are a miracle. God is your Father, and He created you, too. But not in the same way that Jesus was created."

She paused for a moment, trying to figure out how to best explain the conception and birth of Christ. She smiled at the children and plunged on.

"You see, Jesus' mother, Mary, wasn't married when she conceived, so Jesus didn't have an earthly father," she tried to explain.

Joshua, being the oldest and wisest of the group of young children, spoke up and said, "My mom says it's a sin when you have a baby and you're not married."

Miss Lighthart's face flushed a bit. This, the most special story of all time, wasn't coming out quite the way she had planned.

"Well, it wasn't a sin for Mary because she had never known a man," Miss Lighthart patiently explained.

Joshua spoke up again. "If she didn't know any men, then why was she with Joseph? He was a man."

"Yeah," Emma agreed, "and how could she be a mommy without having a daddy?"

"Yeah," a little boy named Cody joined in the argument. "Every baby has a daddy. Someone had to be the dad....."

"Hey," piped up Benjamin. "They were Joseph and Mary just like my grandma and grandpa!"

Miss Lighthart was trying to be patient, but she was starting to feel not only outnumbered, but also as if the story was getting away from her again. The children kept jumping to their own conclusions, and were not allowing her time to explain.

"Jesus did have a father, I mean does have a Father,"

she explained. "God is His Father!"

For a moment, the room was completely silent as the young children tried to process it. Then one little girl spoke up.

"How did that happen?" she asked, looking shyly up at the elderly teacher.

"Like I was saying," Miss Lighthart continued, "It was a miracle."

"Oh, back to the miracle thing again," Joshua grunted.

"Oh, but it was a miracle," Miss Lighthart smiled at him. "The greatest and most important miracle of all time."

The children all just sat quietly at the table and stared at her with blank expressions, so she hurried on with the story.

"And after Mary gave birth to Baby Jesus, she wrapped Him in swaddling clothes and laid Him in a manger," she explained.

Her audience continued to wear blank expressions, and Miss Lighthart feared she had lost their attention. So in an effort to once again involve them in the story, she came up with a plan.

"Let's act the story out," she suggested.

Her audience immediately came to life. They weren't quite sure what she had in mind, but it had to be better than trying to figure out what a miracle was, or how Mary could have a baby without a man.

"Now, who would like to be Mary?" she asked.

Miss Lighthart diligently set to work doling out roles for the nativity scene. Little Emma would be Mary. Her brother, Jacob, would be Joseph. The remainder of the children would portray angels, shepherds, or animals. Joshua chose to be a shepherd while Benjamin wanted to be one of the sheep.

The elderly teacher was delighted with the eagerness of her young students. This would be a fun way to teach them her favorite story. They moved the table and chairs out of the way and began to set up the scene.

"Okay, Mary," Miss Lighthart said. "You sit here and hold the baby."

She handed her a bundle of clothing and moved onto the next person. Little "Mary" looked into the bundle and said, "This isn't a baby. This is just a coat."

"Yes, yes," Miss Lighthart said. "I didn't know we were going to act out the story, so I didn't bring a baby. We will just have to use our imaginations."

She took "Joseph" by the hand and said, "And, Joseph, you stand right here beside Mary."

If Miss Lighthart thought the rest of her students would patiently wait their turn to be placed in the manger scene, she was sadly mistaken. They had already turned into a pack of animals. The cow was chasing a little lamb, while the donkey was kicking and braying. Joshua, as the little shepherd boy, was chasing them around. Whether he was trying to round them up and bring them back to the stable, or chasing them for fun, was not quite clear.

"Children, children," Miss Lighthart said, clearly flustered and distressed. "This is not how the story goes. Remember the song, 'Silent Night?' This was a peaceful, glorious event. What we have here is more like a zoo!"

"I went to the zoo once," Jacob announced. "It was lots of fun!"

"Yeah, I love the zoo!" agreed Joshua.

"Me, too!" chorused little Emma and Benjamin.

It was quite obvious that Miss Lighthart's students were more interested in the zoo scene, with the frolicking antics of wild and unruly animals, than the somber, more peaceful scene from that blissful night years ago in the quiet manger.

****

Meanwhile, Candy and Grandma Mary had been preparing for the morning service with Pastor Ron. Prior to entering the sanctuary, Mary and Candy had paused in the foyer to greet fellow parishioners and hang their coats. Candy was delighted to see old acquaintances and share hugs with long-lost friends.

"Candy!" exclaimed Shelly, one of Candy's old classmates from school. "How are you? I haven't seen you in years!"

They exchanged hugs and Candy was quick to show off her daughter.

"This is my youngest child, Hannah," Candy beamed proudly. "I have two older boys, but they have already gone downstairs to check out the Children's Church program."

Shelly smiled at Hannah and said, "Well, aren't you adorable."

Hannah smiled shyly and replied with a "Thank you," after a prompting from her mother.

"What a beautiful dress," Shelly complimented her. "And with such a pretty bow on the back."

Hannah grinned and Candy said, "Oh, she loves this dress. She will be extremely disappointed when she outgrows it."

She paused, and then added, "I was just telling my dad this morning how it is hard to get her to part with it long enough to just throw it in the laundry." Smiling at her mother, she said, "It was a special gift from her grandmother."

Shelly smiled at Mary, rubbed Hannah's back and said, "Well, Grandma Mary definitely has good taste." Turning to walk away, she said, "I'm going to go find a seat. It was so nice to see you again, Candy!"

"Nice to see you, too," Candy smiled as she waved to her high school friend.

Mary and Candy decided it was time to find seats, too. They made their way into the sanctuary, and who should they meet first but Mary's arch enemy, Margaret Wellington. And, of course, Margaret had to head directly toward them to make her presence known.

"Quick, Candy," Mary urgently whispered. "Let's go sit over there." She practically dragged Candy away.

"What's the rush, Mom?" Candy asked in surprise.

"It's old Maggie Wellington," she whispered. "And I don't feel like talking to her right now."

Candy smiled and said, "Still at odds with her, Mom?"

"I'm not one to get even," Mary smiled, directing Candy to a seat in the opposite direction of Margaret Wellington, "so I guess I will always be 'at odds' with her!"

Candy chuckled at her mother's humor and made her way into her seat. And fortunately for Mary, someone distracted Mrs. Wellington before she could reach them. But before the service began, Margaret made her way up the aisle and seated herself in the row of seats adjacent to them.

"Why can't she just leave us alone?" Mary whispered to her daughter. "Sometimes I feel like she is stalking me."

"Oh, Mom," Candy whispered back. "Don't be so paranoid!"

Mary gave her daughter a sideways glance and raising an eyebrow said, "You think I'm paranoid?"

Candy leaned over and gave her mother a quick kiss on the cheek, just as the service began. She was excited to hear the lively music and festive singing, and even more delighted with how well Hannah was behaving. She didn't always sit well in church, and Candy wasn't sure how she would react to a roomful of strangers. But she seemed to be enjoying the music and all seemed to be going well. And then the music stopped....

The congregation settled down and Pastor Ron began to speak, but little Hannah had either had enough of being quiet, or she just didn't want to listen to what he had to say.

"When are we going home, Mommy?" she asked, making no attempt to lower the volume of her voice.

"Shh!" her mother cautioned her. "Not yet," she whispered, indicating that Hannah should do the same.

Hannah either didn't take the hint, or simply didn't care about being quiet. A few moments later, she spoke up and loudly said, "I want to go to Grandma's house."

Candy again warned her to be quiet. Looking anxiously around her, she noticed Margaret Wellington giving her a phony smile. She gave a brief smile in return before turning her attention back to Pastor Ron. At that moment, Hannah decided she had sat still long enough. She was going to Grandma Mary's house with or without her mother. She quickly climbed out of her mother's lap, made her way past her grandmother, and headed for the nearest aisle.

"Where are you going, Hannah?" Grandma Mary asked her.

Hannah paused for a brief moment as she contemplated her grandmother's question, then matter-of-factly stated, "To your house to see Bumpa!"

And with that, she turned and headed out into the aisle. Grandma Mary was caught off-guard and grabbed for her granddaughter's closest arm. But Hannah was faster than she realized, and all she managed to grab was the big, bright red bow on the back of her dress. There was a terrible tearing noise, and Grandma Mary's expression filled with horror when she realized she had just torn the bow off the back of Hannah's dress.

Hannah stopped in her tracks, looked at her beautiful bow in her grandmother's hand, and then up into the face of her shocked grandmother. There was a moment of silence as she processed what had just happened, and then she threw herself onto the floor and began to wail at the top of her lungs.

Grandma Mary felt terrible. She knew how much that dress, complete with the bow, had meant to Hannah. All she wanted to do was comfort her devastated little granddaughter. But Hannah was not interested in being comforted, especially by the one who had caused her current predicament of pain and despair.

As Grandma Mary bent down to pick her up, Hannah started flailing and kicking. An unfortunate moment of timing found Hannah's shiny black dress shoe making contact with Grandma Mary's right eyebrow. Mary reeled in pain, and poor Candy didn't know who to help first.

But of course, Margaret Wellington was there in an instance, rushing to their aid. The whole congregation seemed to hang in suspense, watching the scene unfold like a bad dream. But leave it to Mrs. Wellington to rescue the situation. She gave a wave to Pastor Ron, letting him know she had everything under control. Then she put an arm around Mary's shoulder and guided her out of the sanctuary, as Candy followed behind with the very distraught Hannah.

Margaret led them down the stairs and into the kitchen in the basement, where she got a cold cloth for Mary.

"We probably should put some ice on that," she stated.

"No, this is fine, Margaret, really," Mary insisted, adjusting the cold cloth over her eye.

Opening the freezer door, Margaret said, "I'm sure there is something in here that we could use." Finding a bag of peas, she added, "Oh, here, this is perfect. Hold this bag of peas over your eye."

Mary really did not care to have Margaret Wellington fussing over her, but she did agree that the frozen peas would probably feel good. So she accepted the gesture and applied the bag to her aching eye. As she did, Margaret headed to the telephone sitting on the counter and picked up the receiver.

"You're not calling rescue, are you?" Mary asked in a panic. "I'll be fine. I just need a few minutes to rest."

"Oh, no," Margaret waved her off. "I'm calling your husband to let him know that you have been injured."

And with that, Margaret dialed the number without even needing to ask Mary what it was.

Mary seethed, instantly feeling her blood pressure rise. She hoped her face didn't display the raging battle taking place inside of her. Margaret's plan was now clear. Not only had she portrayed herself as the heroine by ushering them out of the sanctuary, but she was also using this as an opportunity to contact Mary's husband. There were names for people like Margaret Wellington, but Mary was not known to use them! Plus, they were highly inappropriate to be uttered within the walls of a church.

"You don't need to bother him," Mary insisted. "His back is hurting and he has enough to deal with. He doesn't need to worry about me."

"It's not a problem," Margaret replied. "You don't want

him to be shocked when you walk in with a distorted face, so I'm just trying to prepare him."

Mary removed the bag of peas and stared at it, as if it was a mirror that could reflect the image of her face. She looked at Candy as if to ask, "Do I really look that bad?" but Candy just shook her head and rolled her eyes. Margaret was exaggerating, as usual.

Mary looked at Margaret and, judging by the change in her expression, assumed Joseph had just answered on the other end of the call.

"Hello, Joey," Margaret said, sounding as sweet as pie, "It's Margaret."

There was a brief pause, and then Margaret's face took on a cloudy look.

"Wellington," she added, with a note of disgust in her voice.

Mary quickly turned her head so Margaret wouldn't see the smile that crept across her face. She had to give her husband credit. Margaret was the only one they knew that called him Joey, and they had a limited number of acquaintances named Margaret. But he had put her in her place by pretending to not know who was calling. Mary loved that husband of hers!

Margaret recovered quickly, and bustled on with her tidbit of news. "I'm calling to let you know that your wife has had a bit of a mishap here at the church."

There was a pause, and then she quickly added, "Oh no, you don't need to come get her. She's still mobile, it's just that she has sustained a facial injury. I didn't want you to be shocked when you saw her, that's all. Her face is somewhat distorted."

My goodness, Mary thought to herself, *he's going to thing I look like I got hit by a bus!* It felt a little puffy and was probably coloring, but "distorted" sounded a little extreme.

Margaret finished her phone call and went back to pampering Mary, all the while boasting of her involvement in community activities. She had so many projects to complete, and she simply didn't know how she and the ladies in her organizations would get everything done in time for the holidays.

Mary kept insisting she was fine and really didn't need Margaret fussing over her. She wasn't accustomed to attention like this to begin with, but especially didn't desire it from her arch enemy, not that Margaret was even aware she held that position in Mary's life.

Finally, after what seemed like an eternity, they heard rustling from the sanctuary above. Assuming that church must be over, Mary grabbed the opportunity to rid herself of Mrs. Wellington's unwanted services.

"It sounds like church is ending," she announced. Looking at Candy, she added, "We better go get the boys."

As she gathered her belongings and prepared to leave, she remembered that her daughter, Joy, had wanted her to request help from the ladies of the church for the annual tree lighting ceremony.

"Oh, Margaret," she said, stopping at the kitchen door to turn and face her not-so-favorite friend. "Joy had wanted me to ask if the ladies of the church could help provide some home baked goods for the tree lighting ceremony next week."

Margaret, who had been washing the table and putting the chairs back in place, stopped and looked up with a surprised expression.

"Well, Mary," she began, indignantly, "I'm not so sure about that. I just told you how extremely busy we have been. We have all the gifts to gather, organize, and wrap for the Project CARE program. Plus, we have all the festivities here at the church to plan and prepare for. Not to mention our own family provisions for the holidays. I just don't see how we could possibly have time to add anything more to our already overloaded agendas!"

Mary was caught off-guard by Margaret's response, and struggled to find adequate words to reply. This was a community event for the children and families in all of Enfield and its surrounding towns. She was sure Margaret Wellington would have jumped at the opportunity to be involved with making herself shine a little brighter by at least bringing a batch of cookies.

Mary fumbled for words, and finally said, "Well, if it's too much for you, Margaret, then don't worry about it. We will work it out on our own."

She turned to leave the room, but then realized she was still holding the bag of peas in her hand. For a brief moment, she was tempted to throw it at Margaret. But she caught herself, realizing it would be an immature act and something Pastor Ron wouldn't approve of. So she simply walked over to Margaret, slapped the slightly-thawed bag of peas on the table in front of her, and said, "Thanks for the peas!"

With that, she turned and left the room with Candy and little Hannah. As she headed up the stairs, she looked at Candy and muttered, "Pompous old bitty!"

****

When Mary, Candy, and Hannah arrived at the upper level of the church, they saw that the Children's Church participants were already there. Joshua and Benjamin were acting out, as usual, and Miss Lighthart seemed quite flustered with trying to keep them under control. Candy immediately went to her rescue.

"Boys, that's enough!" Candy scolded them. Looking at Miss Lighthart, she asked, "Did they give you a hard time?"

Miss Lighthart never wanted to give a bad report to a parent. She had worked with children all of her life and knew they had lots of energy which they often struggled to contain. But she was feeling a bit overwhelmed and a little on the grumpy side right now.

Just looking at her expression, Candy knew she had had a rough morning. "I'm so sorry if they were difficult for you," she apologized.

"No problem, they were no problem," Miss Lighthart

mumbled. But she could not make eye contact with Candy. She was a lousy liar, and she knew it. She was quick to excuse herself and wandered off to get her coat, which she promptly donned and exited the building, without so much as a farewell to another person.

Pastor Ron called after her, attempting to inquire about how her class went today. She just waved him off and continued her descent down the church walkway. He raised his eyebrows in surprise. In all his years of pastoring the Enfield Community Church, he couldn't remember this type of behavior from Miss Lighthart before. She would always shake his hand and wish him a blessed week before leaving.

Turning to look around the foyer, Pastor Ron saw Candy and Mary gathering up their offspring. Remembering the upset during the service, he came over to inquire about the status of Mary's face. She had recovered emotionally, but her face bore some bruising, and it looked like she might even sport a black eye.

"How are you doing, Mary?" Pastor Ron inquired.

"I'll be fine," she said, humbly. "I think my pride is hurt more than my face. I'm sorry we were such a disruption during the service."

"Don't you trouble yourself about it," Pastor Ron insisted. "Kids will be kids. We all know they can be totally unpredictable."

Just then, they heard squealing tires coming from the direction of the parking lot. The group rushed to the front door, concerned that a crash was about to follow. The parishioners were shocked to see Miss Lighthart squealing out of the yard.

"Wow! It looks like Miss Lighthart is anxious to get home today," Pastor Ron observed.

"Oh, no," sighed Candy. "I don't think it's necessarily that she is anxious to get home, just anxious to get away from here, and my boys. I'm afraid they were too much for her today."

Pastor Ron chuckled and put his hand on Candy's shoulder. "Don't you worry about Miss Lighthart. She may be feeling a little heavy-hearted right now," he paused and chuckled at his wit, then continued, "but she usually bounces back pretty quickly. She'll probably be good as gold by next week."

"Or ready to retire," Candy added.

Mary hugged her daughter's shoulder and said, "I'll give her a call later this week to make sure she is okay. And maybe make her a batch of cookies as a peace treaty!"

Mary and her daughter rounded up the restless boys, said their good-byes to Pastor Ron, and headed home so they could check on Grandpa Joseph. Once in the car, the conversation turned to the events of the week. Mary shared with Candy about how Joey's bird died, how some of her souvenirs from the European vacation had been broken, and the tubing adventure yesterday that left Grandpa Joseph incapacitated in his easy chair this morning.

"Sounds like you have had quite a week," Candy commented.

"True enough," Mary agreed. "This hasn't been as easy as I thought it would be."

"Who comes tomorrow?" Candy asked, adding, "Maybe you will have an easier day."

"Nicholas is due tomorrow," Mary answered. Pausing a moment, she added, "Hopefully it will be a quieter day, since he only has Mackenzie. Being just four years old and a girl, she shouldn't be too much trouble."

"Not like my gang," Candy commented. Mary and Candy stopped to listen to the commotion coming out of the back seat. There was definitely a lot of energy back there.

"Your boys are fine," Mary smiled. "They're just boys with lots of energy. I raised six of them, so I know what boys are like."

Looking in the rearview mirror, she said, "Settle down boys. We are almost home, and then we will have some lunch with Grandpa Joseph."

She turned her attention back to the conversation with Candy. "My only concern tomorrow is with Morgan. I wear my heart on my sleeve, and I am not good at hiding my true feelings. Morgan has not been known to be my favorite daughter-in-law.”

"Aw, yes,” Candy agreed. "She can be challenging. She always looks like she just climbed out of a fashion magazine. Never a hair out of place or a wrinkle in her clothing, or Nick’s, for that matter! She is the picture of perfection.”

"And me, on the other hand…” Mary paused and shot her daughter a sideways glance, "I raised twelve kids and didn’t have time for perfection. I was lucky if I remembered to brush my own hair. And it’s too late to start seeking perfection now!”

Candy chuckled and said, "So very true.”

She reached over to pat her mother’s arm and said, "But you have had to learn to go with the flow through the years, Mom. So tomorrow, just float along with it!”

****

****

Nicholas

****

Chapter 9
Nicholas

☆☆☆☆☆☆☆

On Day Eight, Nicholas and his family arrived promptly at the appointed time. Morgan was not known to be late, not by a minute. Perfection simply was not an option for Morgan. It was the way she lived her life.

Mary had decorated the front door with a handmade picture of St. Nick. Nicholas smiled at his mother's inventiveness. She had always been so crafty, creating works of art from leftovers and scraps.

"Who's that, Daddy?" Mackenzie asked, pointing at the picture of St. Nick on the door.

"That is St. Nick," Nicholas explained with a smile on his face. "You remember the song we sing about Jolly Old St. Nicholas? This is what he looks like."

"Sort of," Morgan snorted. "This St. Nick looks a little scruffy."

Nick glanced over at his beautiful wife, but he knew from experience not to contradict her. He hesitated before replying, then picked Mackenzie up and said, "That's okay. Mackenzie and I like him just the way he is."

He gave his daughter a quick hug and said, "Ready to go see Grandma Mary and Grandpa Joseph?"

"Uh-huh," she nodded. "And Grandma can read to me!"

Nick looked at Mackenzie's new book, tucked securely under her arm, and said, "Grandma would love to read to you. Do you want to ring the doorbell?"

Just inside the door, Grandma Mary was busily preparing for their arrival. Knowing what a perfectionist Morgan was, she had been making last minute adjustments, trying to assure that everything was in its proper place. She

130

had been up early to vacuum and dust, attempting to free her house of every visible speck of imperfection. She had even washed windows and dusted every corner to remove the cobwebs which had managed to accumulate there. Grandpa Joseph chuckled as he watched her.

"I don't think this place has ever been this clean," he smiled at his wife.

"Sure it has," she smiled back at him. Turning her attention back toward an exceptionally ugly cobweb, she said over her shoulder, "It was this clean the day we moved in a few decades ago!"

Joseph shook his head and gave his wife another smile. He thought she looked kind of cute with the shiner Hannah had given her in church yesterday, but he knew Mary had been horrified when she looked in the mirror that morning.

"What do you think Morgan will think about your black eye?" he asked.

Mary groaned. "Doesn't it figure that the day "Miss Perfection" is coming to visit, I have to have a black eye!"

Joseph, still not fully recovered from the sledding escapade, hobbled over to give his wife a hug and kiss on the forehead.

"I think it looks kind of cute," he smiled down at her.

"I'm sure Morgan will not find it 'cute.' She will probably be repulsed by my lack of perfection and won't want to be seen in public with me." Mary groaned again and buried her face in her husband's chest.

Just then the doorbell rang. It startled Mary and Joseph, who hadn't realized their company had arrived.

"Oh, no," Mary exclaimed. "I didn't realize they were already here. I hope they didn't hear me."

Joseph smiled and gave his wife another reassuring hug. "I don't think they heard you, Mary. Just stay calm today, and try not to make any waves with Morgan."

Mary returned the hug and said, "I'll try not to. But she has a way of getting under my skin and irritating me. Kind of like scabies."

Joseph chuckled and gave his wife a playful pat on the behind. "Oh, come on," he said. "She isn't that bad."

Mary went to answer the door, turning to her husband with a raised eyebrow and a skeptical smile. She would do her best, but….. Mary turned on the charm and opened the door, determined to greet her not-so-favorite daughter-in-law with a smile on her face, forced or otherwise. But just as she had anticipated, the bad vibrations began almost immediately.

She greeted Nicholas with a hug and a kiss, which was returned with open and honest affection. The same was true with Mackenzie. But when she turned to greet Morgan, the look of disgust was quite obvious.

"What happened to your eye?" Morgan inquired dryly.

Mary took a breath and tried to remain calm. She didn't want to get off on the wrong foot, and maybe she had misread Morgan's expression.

"Oh, it's nothing serious," Mary brushed it off. "My face just had an unfortunate encounter with Hannah's foot yesterday at church."

She gave a brief summary of the event, made light of it, and shrugged it off. Grandma Mary turned her attention to little Mackenzie, reaching out to take her from Nick. As she did, she heard Morgan comment from behind her.

"Well, I wanted to go to the mall today," she said, "but we can't go with you looking like that."

As Grandma Mary settled Mackenzie on her hip, she could see her husband watching her from over her granddaughter's head. She arched an eyebrow and gave him a sideways smirk, as if to say, I'm biting my tongue, Joseph!

"Look at how big you are," Grandma Mary said, hugging Mackenzie and showering her with kisses.

Mackenzie giggled, then pulled her book out from under her arm and asked, "Will you read my new book to me, Grandma?"

Grandma Mary took the book offered by her beautiful, little granddaughter and said, "I would love to read it to you. Let's go sit in Grandpa Joseph's easy chair."

She helped Mackenzie remove her winter clothing and hung it in the closet. Then the two of them settled down into Grandpa's easy chair to read the story. Grandpa Joseph, realizing he had been silently excused, escorted Nick and Morgan to the kitchen for a cup of coffee.

Mackenzie's new book was a classic Christmas tale, telling about Santa's Christmas Eve sleigh ride and coming down the chimney to deliver presents to all the good little boys and girls. Mackenzie sat quietly in Grandma Mary's lap and listened intently while she read. As soon as the story was finished, the questions began.

"How did Santa fit down the "chimbally"?" she asked, followed by, "Doesn't he get burned?" and "Won't the presents get burned?" along with "How does he know he's at the right house?"

Grandma Mary did her best to answer Mackenzie's multitude of questions.   Just as she was running out of explanations, Mackenzie changed her focus.

"You have a fireplace," she commented, looking across the living room at Grandma Mary's fireplace.

"Yes, we do," Grandma Mary smiled down at her.

"Did you have to put your fire out so Santa could come down your "chimbally"?" Mackenzie inquired.

"Oh, of course," Grandma Mary grinned at her inquisitive little granddaughter. "We didn't want Santa to get burned."

"Does he still come out your fireplace?" she continued with her inquiries.

"Oh, no," Grandma Mary explained. "We don't have any children living here anymore."

She hesitated, and then added with a chuckle, "Plus, he would get way too dirty coming through that old fireplace. Grandpa Joseph hasn't cleaned it in a very long time."

At that moment, Morgan appeared at the living room door.

"Are you almost done with that story?" she asked. "We are going to be late for the mall."

"Just finished," Grandma Mary said, giving Mackenzie

a kiss on the head and setting her on the floor.

Grandpa Joseph and Nick followed Morgan into the living room.

"Are we going to head to the mall now?" Nick asked, looking at his wife for direction.

Morgan glanced from Nick to his mother, and then said, "I have to try to fix your mother's eye before we go. Give me a minute to run out to the car and get my make-up kit."

Mary wanted to groan. *She really carries her make-up with her at all times?* she thought. *Most of the time, I don't even wear make-up!*

She watched Morgan hurry out the front door. Then, speaking quietly to avoid being overheard by Mackenzie, she said, "I hope this doesn't take too long. We don't want Morgan to be late for the mall!"

Nick knew his mother didn't see eye-to-eye with his wife, and he often had to play mediator. With Morgan out of hearing range, Nick smiled knowingly at his mother and simply stated, "Heaven forbid that we stand between Morgan and a shopping expedition to the mall!"

Morgan returned with her make-up kit and directed Mary to the kitchen. The lighting was better there and allowed more room to work. While they were occupied, Joseph decided to show Nick some of the projects he had been working on during his retirement. Little Mackenzie climbed up into Bumpa's easy chair and decided to review her book again.

With Morgan's expertise in applying make-up, it didn't take long to cover all of the colorful markings associated with Mary's black eye. When they were done, Mary excused herself to finish getting ready to leave. While Morgan set about packing up her kit, Mary ran to her bedroom mirror to scrutinize her face. She was not sure she trusted her daughter-in-law, and wanted to make sure she hadn't made her look like a lady of the night.

Not more than a few minutes had passed when everyone was startled to hear a blood-curdling scream. It seemed to be coming from the living room, so the adults all charged that way with a sense of urgency. But when they arrived, it quickly became clear that it wasn't an emergency at all, to anyone but Morgan, that is. A look of horror definitely covered Morgan's face, but after assessing the situation, it was hard for Mary to stifle her desire to laugh.

Having been left to entertain herself, Mackenzie had decided to get a closer view of the fireplace. Apparently she had decided it was much too dirty for Santa to use, so she had taken it upon herself to clean it up. So there she stood, wearing her perfect little outfit, but covered from head-to-toe with a layer of black, disgusting soot.

Morgan almost looked paralyzed with fear. She had never seen her child so dirty before. But worse than that, as her mother, it was her responsibility to clean her up. She probably feared that some of the soot would transfer to her! The look on Morgan's face, as well as Mackenzie's current condition, were almost more than Mary could take. She had to leave the room before she burst into laughter.

She ran to the kitchen and grabbed a roll of paper towels, as if that would be of any help, and came hurrying back to the living room. She knew the paper towels were useless in this situation, but retrieving them had given her a moment to compose herself. She rushed into the living room and donned a look of concern.

"Oh, dear, what happened here?" she questioned her granddaughter. "We need to get you cleaned up so we can go to the mall."

Naturally, Morgan had brought another perfect little outfit for Mackenzie, just in case she should get a spot of dirt on the one she had worn. But this was more than just a spot. Mary could see that Morgan did not wish to touch the sooty little girl that stood before them, so while Nick went to retrieve the clean outfit from the car, she helped her to the bathroom and began to fill the bathtub. Once the sooty clothes were removed and Mackenzie was safely placed in the bathtub, Morgan was quick to take over and scrub her up.

Before heading to the bathroom to clean her daughter

up, Morgan had instructed Nicholas to finish cleaning the fireplace out so this would not happen again. After she exited the room, Grandpa Joseph reassured him that he didn't need to clean his dirty fireplace. Grandpa would clean it when they got back from the mall. But Nick knew his wife well, and said it would be better for everyone if he just did it now and got it over with. To cross Morgan usually meant an uncomfortable night on the couch!

So while Morgan was bathing Mackenzie, and Nicholas was cleaning the fireplace, Mary and Joseph retreated to the kitchen for a moment of reprieve.

"How can you be late for the mall?" Mary whispered to her husband, while she washed the coffee cups in the sink. Turning to look at him over her shoulder, she added, "And who's making us late for the mall now?"

Joseph took a final sip from his coffee cup, got up to place it in the sink, and kissed his wife on the head. "It's only one day, Mary. You can do this."

"I know," Mary sighed, "but it has the potential to be one very long day!"

****

Much to Mary's amazement, the rest of the day went very well. The mall was beautifully decorated for the holidays, with a seasonal North Pole display where children could have their picture taken with Santa. A special Christmas train circled the interior of the mall, so Grandma Mary and Grandpa Joseph took a ride with Mackenzie while Nick and Morgan rested on one of the benches.

Mackenzie looked so cute, with her recent makeover at her grandparent's house, so Mary and Joseph decided it was worth taking the time to stand in line to have her picture taken with Santa. Mackenzie was good as gold while she patiently waited for her turn on Santa's lap. And when her turn finally arrived, she told him all about how she had cleaned the "chimbally" for him, so he wouldn't get dirty at Grandma Mary's house.

Mary was actually enjoying herself, surprisingly enough. She had dreaded this day more than the other eleven, not feeling sure that she could keep herself from saying something to Morgan that she would regret. But this had been a successful event, proving to be much better than the events of the past few days. Nothing had been broken. No one had been injured. Everything was going great. And then she turned the corner and came face-to-face with Margaret Wellington.

Mary's first thought was to turn around quickly and pretend she hadn't seen her. She thought to herself, *That woman is a thorn in my flesh. Can't I go anywhere without bumping into her?*

But turning to flee was not an option. Margaret seemed delighted to see them, and was not about to let them get away without a greeting.

"Mary! Joey!" she declared. "It's so good to see you."

She stared intently at Mary, as if doing a thorough inspection of her face, trying to find signs of bruising from yesterday's episode at church. Not accustomed to wearing make-up, Mary had unknowingly smudged the cover-up Morgan had applied. It was clearly in need of repair, and Margaret naturally thought it was her Christian duty to let Mary know.

"I see that you have tried to cover your shiner," Margaret said, with a note of disapproval in her tone. "But it's clear to see you are not familiar with applying make-up, because it simply wasn't done properly."

Mary looked from Morgan to Margaret, not quite sure what to say. One of the women before her was a perfectionist, while the other was just plain cruel. And quite frankly, Mary didn't care what it looked like anyway. She wasn't the one who had to look at it!

Yet, to say the wrong thing at a moment like this could be disastrous. With the wrong comment, either party could become very upset and cause an ugly scene. So, there she stood, tongue-tied, while she searched the recesses of her brain trying to figure out what to do next. She was very surprised when Morgan came to her rescue.

"She didn't put her make-up on," Morgan stated matter-of-factly. "I did it. I didn't want her to be embarrassed about sporting a shiner in a public place, especially when it was caused while trying to be a good grandmother."

She glanced at Mary and added, "But it does look like it is time for a refresher."

Morgan smiled at her mother-in-law, who gave her a genuine smile in return. And this time, it was Margaret Wellington who was tongue-tied.

"Oh, yes, well....," she stuttered, and then quickly added, "It does look like it is time for a refresher."

She quickly excused herself, stating she had more shopping to do and didn't have time to chat. Morgan and Mary watched her walk off, while Joseph and Nick were less obvious about it, appearing to be intently showing Mackenzie something in the storefront window across the corridor.

"Who was that lady?" Morgan asked.

"I'm not sure 'lady' is the correct term for her," Mary smiled, "but she is someone sent to Earth to make my life miserable."

They chuckled and Morgan put an arm around her mother-in-law's shoulder.

"Your eye doesn't really look that bad," she whispered. "It just sounded like she needed to be put in her place."

"Well, thank you, I appreciate that," Mary smiled back at her daughter-in-law.

"But why don't we go to the restroom and do a bit of a touch-up," Morgan suggested, "just in case we bump into her again. We want to be prepared!"

Mary just looked at her and smiled. She had never seen the compassionate side of Morgan before.

Morgan turned to the trio checking out the Christmas décor across the corridor and called over to them, "We'll be right back. We are heading to the restroom for a touch up."

She linked her arm through her mother-in-law's and headed off down the long main corridor of the all-too-familiar mall. As they walked, she chatted and laughed with her mother-in-law.

"Did you see her face when I told her it was my cover-up job?" Morgan chatted. "She was trying to insult you and it backfired on her."

Mary smiled and said, "Thanks for coming to my rescue. She frustrates me, and I'm never quite sure how to handle her."

Morgan leaned over and rubbed shoulders with her mother-in-law. "Well, I didn't have any trouble handling her!"

"So true," Mary agreed. "You handled her just fine."

"No one is going to insult my mother-in-law!" Morgan stated.

Mary looked at Morgan, eyes wide with surprise. She squeezed her hand and said, "Well, thank you for that."

After reaching the restroom, the pair set up a mini cosmetology shop. Mary was nothing short of amazed at the amount of make-up Morgan carried in her purse. Mary had probably never even owned that much make-up in her entire life!

While Morgan worked, Mary gave her more details of how Hannah had accidentally kicked her in the face during the church service yesterday, and how Margaret Wellington had naturally felt it her duty to come to their rescue. And then how Mary had wanted to throw the bag of peas at her for her attitude. They chatted and laughed like they had been best friends all of their lives.

When they had successfully repaired Mary's wounded face and covered every sign of coloring, they returned to the shopping expedition. They found their husbands and Mackenzie saving a table for them in the food court. They decided to have a bite to eat, and then return to Grandma and Grandpa's house for dessert. Grandma Mary told them how she still had some chocolate éclairs that Cassandra had made, and there were too many for her and Grandpa to eat alone. They could definitely use some help eating all those eclairs that Cassandra had left behind.

****

Back at home, Grandma Mary made another cup of coffee for the adults and hot chocolate for Mackenzie. They settled on the stools at Grandpa Joseph's new island since Mackenzie wanted to sit on the "high" chairs.

They were having a nice chat when Grandpa Joseph looked out the window over the sink and acquired a strange look on his face. He stood up, still looking out the window, then moved closer to the sink for another look.

"Where's my recycling center?" he asked.

"Joseph," Mary chuckled, thinking he was making some kind of a joke. "Do you really think it just got up and walked away?!"

"Well, it's not there," he insisted.

"And where, exactly, would it go?" Mary persisted.

Seeing Joseph's concerned look, the remaining adults got up and joined him at the window. They each scoured the backyard, trying to focus on the recycling center. But no matter how hard they strained to look, they just couldn't bring it into focus.

Morgan helped Mackenzie off her chair, and the group exited the back door for a closer look. They crossed the length of the back yard, but once they reached the spot where Grandpa Joseph's new recycling center once stood, they found nothing but a pile of fresh ashes.

"What the heck?" Grandpa Joseph asked.

"Uh-oh," said Nick.

All eyes quickly focused on his clearly embarrassed face. He looked from one person to another, and then offered an explanation for the missing recycling center.

"I dumped the ashes from the fireplace into your recycling center," he explained. "There must have been a hot ember in there."

This time it was Joseph who didn't know what to say. He had worked hard to build that recycling center, and had been very proud of the final product. And his "To-Do" list seemed to be growing daily. But on the other hand, it was just a wooden box. And Nicholas hadn't meant any harm. To make a big scene about it now would make him feel bad and spoil the day.

"Guess I will just have to add a new recycling center to my list for Santa to bring," Grandpa Joseph said, smiling down at his cute little granddaughter.

Mackenzie looked up at her grandfather and returned the smile. Then she innocently said, "But, Poppa Joe, you're too big to get presents from Santa. You'll just have to go to the mall and buy yourself a new one!"

****

Later that evening, Joy called to check in with her mother. Joy was making final plans for the tree lighting ceremony to be held on the town common in a few days. Mary had agreed to assist her with snacks and decorations, so Joy was checking in to make sure they had everything in place.

Mary gave her the bad news that Margaret Wellington and the ladies from the church would not be able to help with the baked goods. But the two ladies decided they would make what they could. And what they didn't have time for, they would simply have to purchase.

"Nothing wrong with 'almost homemade' treats, right?" Mary chuckled.

After resolving tree lighting issues, Joy asked, "Who came to visit today?"

"Today was Nick's day," Mary replied. "We went to the mall, of course."

Joy chuckled and said, "Knowing Morgan, I probably could have guessed as much. How did everything go?"

"It turned out to be a good day," Mary admitted. "Much better than I expected. Morgan and I actually bonded some today."

"Is that right?" Joy asked, the surprise clearly resounding in her voice. She knew that her mother had always struggled with her feelings for Morgan.

Mary shared the events of the day with Joy, finishing up with the death of Joseph's recycling center.

"It seems like your father has a growing 'To-Do' list," Mary sighed. "He'll have plenty of work to do once we make it through the holidays."

The conversation turned to the events of the next few days. Mary told Joy she only had a few more days left before she had entertained all twelve of her children. Tomorrow she would do the live nativity with Angel's family, and the following day they were going to try skiing with Berry.

"I haven't skied for years," Mary said nervously.

"It's like riding a bike, Mom," Joy insisted. "Once you learn, you never forget."

"I hope you're right," her mother replied. "I almost told Berry we couldn't go, but I know he wants to show off his ski resort. He is so excited about it. I decided to give it a try so as not to disappoint him."

"Well, good luck, Mom," Joy wished her mother well. "Just don't overdo it. You can always hang out in the lodge by the fireplace."

"That sounds good to me," Mary smiled at the thought. "Maybe I'll fake a backache, bring a good book, and just relax by the fire."

"You couldn't do that, Mom," Joy stated. "You always have to be in the middle of the action."

"You know me too well," Mary grinned. "Maybe I'm just too nosy."

"Not nosy," Joy corrected, "just busy and involved."

"I guess so," Mary agreed.

"But if you want to know what 'nosy' looks like," Joy went on, "there's always Margaret Wellington!"

"Oh!" groaned Mary, "definitely nosy. Very involved, but way too nosy!"

"Good old Haggie Maggie," Joy chuckled.

"Joy!" Mary scolded playfully. "I raised you better than that. You should know better than to call people names!"

"I call them the way I see them," Joy laughed, quoting an old saying her mother used to say frequently.

"And you see her as a hag?" Mary laughed back, unable to stifle the chuckle.

"All right," Joy corrected herself. "How about Naggie Maggie? She is a bit of a nag."

"Well, I guess I can't argue with that," Mary replied. "She does nag until she gets her way. That's why she is playing Mrs. Claus at the tree lighting instead of me."

"She only wanted to play Mrs. Claus so she could pretend she is married to Dad," laughed Joy. "You know that as well as I do."

"She is so infatuated with your father," Mary agreed. "But she can't have him. He's mine, and I'm not willing to part with him."

"I don't think Dad would want 'Naggie Maggie' anyway, Mom," Joy chuckled.

Mary smiled and replied, "You're terrible, Joy. Didn't your mother ever teach you any manners?"

"She did indeed," Joy cheerfully replied, "but I am an adult now and make my own decisions."

There was a pause in the conversation, then Joy added, "And now I am deciding to end this conversation before my mother lectures me again about name-calling!"

Both ladies laughed and Joy said, "Have fun with Angel tomorrow, and don't worry about skiing with Berry. You'll do fine."

"Keep your fingers crossed for me," Mary requested. Then before hanging up the phone, she added, "Oh, and Joy, don't forget to call 'Naggie Maggie' to make sure she'll be plump enough to fit into her costume!"

"Now who's calling the kettle black?!" Joy laughed as

she hung up the phone.

Mary smiled to herself as she hung up the phone. She didn't know if she was 'a black kettle,' but perhaps she was being just a bit hypocritical!

****

****

Angel

****

Chapter 10
Angel

✫✫✫✫✫✫✫

Mary awoke on Day Nine feeling a little under the weather. It wasn't that she was feeling particularly ill. More likely, it was due to the fact that she was just plain tired. She had forgotten how much work it was to keep up with twelve kids, and having them come one day at a time had not been as easy as she had expected. Her twelve day plan had sounded so perfect on paper, but she was clearly feeling the effects of it now, and she still had a couple of days to get through.

Today will be fun, though, she told herself, trying to coax herself out of the comfort of her bed. Tonight they would go to the live nativity with Angel and her family, and it would be enjoyable watching Davey participate in it. Plus, this would be an evening event, so Angel and her family would not be arriving until shortly before dinner time. That would give Mary most of the day to rest, relax, and have a little renewal time.

Angel had only been in the maternity ward once, but had proudly come home bearing two sons – twin boys whom she had named David and Jonathan. In Biblical times, David and Jonathan had been the best of friends. Angel had hoped her boys would be best friends, too, but on most days they were anything but best friends. They fought constantly, each continuously trying to prove who was bigger and stronger than the other. And since they were identical twins, it was a battle that neither would ever win.

Davey had asked to be a shepherd boy in the live nativity, but Johnny had not wanted to participate this year. It was mostly due to the fact that he didn't particularly care for animals. He felt they were too big and smelly, and feared he would have an encounter with a stray pile of their disgusting discharge. So this year, he had opted to keep his distance

146

and watch with his family from the safety of the audience.

Angel arrived with her family shortly before 3:00 pm. Her boys fought their way from the backseat of the car to the front door, pushing and shoving as they raced to see who could get there first. They arrived almost exactly at the same time, and promptly began to argue over who would ring the doorbell. With the commotion her boys were causing, Angel only briefly got to glimpse the scenery her mother had placed on the door. It was naturally a heavenly angel in white, holding a harp of gold and sporting a glorious halo. Reaching down to break up the fist-wielding battle between her twin boys, Angel had to smirk. She might be an angel, but ironically enough, she had given birth to two little devils!

Mary had heard them coming and opened the door to find Angel in between her swinging sons, looking quite frazzled.

Startled to see the door open, Angel looked up wearily at her mother and said, "I should have been a referee!"

"Looks like you already are, sweetie," her mother replied lightheartedly.

"Grandma!" both boys shouted, forgetting the battle at hand and turning to embrace her.

Grandma Mary greeted her battling grandsons with showers of affection, and then turned her attention to her worn-out daughter.

"Come in, Angel," she told her. "I'll keep the boys occupied for awhile and you can sit down and chat with your father. Then we'll have something to eat before we head to the church for the live nativity."

Looking over her shoulder, Mary asked, "Where's Max?"

"He went to the church already," Angel said, in explanation of her husband's absence. "They needed help setting up the staging. He said he would join us for supper, and then we can all go to the church together."

"Sounds like a plan," Mary agreed.

Davey and Johnny spotted their grandfather standing

in the living room and rushed over to share some hugs with him. Getting carried away as usual, they quickly tackled him to the floor. The trio playfully rolled and wrestled in front of the fireplace. But Grandpa Joseph, fearing the condition of his back, gave up only after a few minutes of play. Davey and Johnny just couldn't seem to let it go, though. Soon enough, their playful wrestling match once again turned into a full-fledged battle.

"That's enough, boys," Angel warned her sons.

Grandma Mary headed their way, intending to step in and physically break up the fight. She was used to brawling boys, having raised a half dozen of her own. Plus they were getting dangerously close to the end table that hosted her Tiffany lamp, and she didn't want anything to happen to that.

But before she could get there, disaster struck. Davey's leg caught the front leg of the table. The momentum was enough to wobble the table and send the lamp toppling to the floor.

Mary closed her eyes in horror and waited for the crash. She silently prayed that it wouldn't come and that someone would miraculously catch the lamp in flight before it landed in pieces on the floor. But this was not a day for miracles. A brief moment later, the dreaded crash came as the lamp all too quickly struck the living room floor.

The fight immediately came to a halt. Realizing how quiet it had become, Mary slowly opened her eyes. But she couldn't bring herself to look at her lamp. Instead, she looked from face-to-face; first Joseph, then Angel, and finally Davey and Johnny, still lying on the floor. Each pair of eyes was focused on her, and they all bore the same expression – pure horror. Judging by their expressions, she knew her lamp could not have fared well.

"David Joseph and Jonathan Maxwell!" their mother scolded. "Get over here and sit on this couch right now!"

Both boys quickly complied with their mother's request. Hearing their middle names always meant that they were in serious trouble. Angel spaced the boys apart, at opposite ends of the couch, and instructed them to not even look at each other. Then she turned her attention to her mother's fractured Tiffany lamp scattered in fragments on the floor.

Grandpa Joseph had already begun picking up some of the pieces to examine them.

"I might be able to fix it, Mary," he said quietly.

Grandma Mary dropped dejectedly into her husband's recliner. It was almost too much. First her cuckoo clock had been broken, then her vase from Vienna, and now her Tiffany lamp, too. All her prize possessions which she had so painstakingly transported home from their once-in-a-lifetime trip to Europe had met their demise at the hands of her children and grandchildren.

"Mom, I'm so sorry," Angel said, looking close to tears herself. "I can have them save their allowance to pay for it, but I know it won't be the same."

Mary felt totally defeated and wanted to give up. She had held it together for the first nine days and managed to salvage each day, no matter what calamity had come along. Deep inside she knew she only had a few days left, and she didn't want Angel's day to be ruined either. Plus, they still had to go to the live nativity.

She was exhausted – physically, emotionally and mentally. But she had to hold it together because Angel deserved a special day, too. *Angel, of all people*, she thought to herself. *She has to deal with this kind of behavior every day. So I should be able to get through one night of it.* So, Mary resolved to worry about her Tiffany lamp later, and blindly move forward from here.

"Can you just put it in a box for now, Joseph?" she asked quietly. "We'll check it out later. Let me just go pull myself together, and I'll be back in a few minutes."

She retreated to the bathroom, where she stopped to take a few deep breaths and splashed some cold water on her face. *Whatever possessed me to have twelve children in the first place*, she muttered to herself. *Why did I have to love my husband so much?!*

After giving herself a few minutes to recover, she made her way back into the living room. There was still an air of gloominess hovering, and there was not a sound to be heard. Joseph had put what was left of the lamp into a box and brought it out to his workshop to deal with later. David and Jonathan still sat quietly on the couch, hands in their laps, with heads hung low. After Mary had left the room, their mother had given them the scolding of a lifetime. Angel sat perched on the edge of her father's recliner, looking anxious and unsure about what she should do.

When Mary stepped into the room, all eyes turned her way. Mary could have read a dozen emotions in their eyes – sorrow, sadness, fear, anxiety – anything but the joy and happiness she wanted to see there. She knew she was the key factor here, and what she did next would either make or break the rest of the day. She could mope about her broken lamp, continue the scolding, and create scars that could last a lifetime. Or she could be positive, let go of the tension, and instead create some fond, family memories. And naturally, being Mary, she chose the latter.

"Does anyone want pizza?" she asked cheerfully. "I thought maybe we could make pizza for supper before heading to the church."

The boys' countenances immediately changed. Relief flooded their faces and the look of sorrow was replaced by joy.

"Does this mean you're not mad at us, Grandma?" Davey asked.

Mary looked lovingly at her grandsons and said, "Come over here, boys."

She sat in an overstuffed chair and motioned for them to come join her. The boys looked at their mother, who nodded her head toward their grandmother. Both boys got up and sheepishly walked over to their grandmother.

Grandma Mary pulled them close and put an arm around each waist. Tenderly, she shared her heart with them.

"That lamp was very special to me," she explained. "That was a souvenir from a very special trip that Grandpa

Joseph and I took, and it is something that I will probably never be able to replace. But let me ask you a question."

She paused, and both boys looked at her intensely. "Did you break that lamp on purpose, or was it an accident?"

Both boys immediately shook their heads in the negative and simultaneously replied, "It was an accident!"

Grandma Mary nodded, and said, "Exactly. You didn't want to see it broken anymore than I did. It was an accident, and that's what accidents are: something that wasn't supposed to happen."

The boys seemed to process this information, like they had never really thought about the definition of "accident" before.

Then Grandma Mary continued. "So, how can I be mad at you for something you didn't mean to do? But here is a piece of advice. You should always look around before you start playing rough to make sure there isn't anything breakable in the way."

Feeling they were getting off pretty easy, both boys looked brightly at their grandmother and smiled.

Johnny reached up to give her a hug and said, "We'll be more careful next time, Grandma."

Following his brother's example, Davey hugged his grandmother as well, and added, "Yeah, we promise!"

Angel looked lovingly at her mother, deeply appreciating her ability to forgive in such a painful situation.

"Pizza time!" Grandma Mary said. She stood and ushered the group into the kitchen.

Soon the kitchen was busy with activity, all three generations working diligently on making pizzas. The boys had flour up to their elbows, with blotches like polka dots on their faces. Grandma Mary laughed joyfully with them and got her camera out to take pictures.

For a brief period of time, the boys seemed to forget their contest to conquer and achieve, and just enjoyed being themselves, while making a horrible mess of Grandma Mary's kitchen in the process.

Grandpa Joseph returned from his workshop, where he had been contemplating his ability to save his wife's Tiffany lamp, and smiled smugly at the laughter coming from the kitchen. His wife was a saint, there was no doubt about it. Even though the last of her souvenirs had just reached its downfall, she was able to move past it and focus on what really mattered – family and good times together.

He wandered out to the kitchen to join them, but was taken by surprise at the horrific mess. Flour not only covered the countertop of his handmade island, but had spilled onto the floor and seemed to have coated each of the boys.

"What is going on in here?" he asked cheerfully.

All four faces turned his way, and pure joy and happiness were written on each one.

"We're making pizza, Grandpa!" Davey explained.

"Yeah. for supper," Johnny added.

Grandpa Joseph smiled fondly and asked, "Are you sure there's some pizza in there? All I see is a mess!" Joseph paused, then remembering a previous day when the kitchen was coated with flour, he added, "Or did your grandmother throw flour at you? She does that sometimes!"

Joseph smiled at his wife and winked. She returned the smile, but said nothing. The twins did not respond, only looking up briefly with a curious expression while continuing to stir their dough. So Joseph added, "Maybe it snowed in here!"

"It's not snow, Grandpa," Davey grinned. "It's flour!"

"Yeah, for the dough," Johnny explained.

"So does that make you flour boys?" Grandpa Joseph smiled in return, reaching over to tousle their hair. The boys grinned back at their grandfather and Joseph proceeded over to his wife. Putting an arm around her, he kissed her on the top of her head. She smiled lovingly up at him, and again, he was reminded of what a special woman he had married.

After finishing the dough, Grandma Mary showed the boys how to spread the sauce and cheese on top. They popped it into the oven and Angel went to clean the boys up while Mary worked on cleaning the kitchen.

Angel's husband, Max, arrived just as they were taking the pizza out of the oven.

"Perfect timing, as usual," Angel said, greeting him with a kiss. Turning to her parents, she explained, "He always seems to show up at the same time as the food."

They all chuckled and proceeded to the table to eat. But as soon as the family entered the dining room and approached the dinner table, the battling warriors returned.

"I'm sitting next to Grammy," Johnny said, rushing over to the chair beside his grandmother.

"No! I'm sitting next to her," Davey insisted, trying to push his brother out of the way.

"Boys!" Angel and Max called out simultaneously.

"I have two sides," Grandma Mary announced, trying to resolve the issue. "I'll sit in the middle and that way you can both sit beside me."

Davey and Johnny seemed happy with that solution, and it seemed like dinner was going to proceed without incident. But it never took much for a battle to begin, and to make it through an entire meal without a struggle was simply expecting too much.

As usual, it began with two twin boys arguing about which was stronger and who was faster. Johnny insisted that he could ride his bike faster than Davey, but Davey was not to be reckoned with. He could ride his bike just as fast as Johnny, and he knew it.

The difference with this battle was that Grandma Mary was located centrally between the battling boys. Not only were they trying to battle around her, but she became the unwilling recipient of a few misguided blows.

"That's enough, boys," Max scolded, jumping up from his place at the table to come separate them. "Maybe someone needs to take a time-out."

Reaching Johnny first, he started to pick him up to remove him from the table. Johnny, feeling he was no more to blame than Davey, and the unwanted recipient of a punishment, was not interested in leaving the table.

"No!" he screamed. "I want to stay here with Grandma!"

Angel got up to remove Davey, who was located on the other side of Grandma Mary. But Davey was no more interested in a time-out or being taken away from his place beside his grandmother, than was his twin brother.

"Do you think Grandma Mary wants you boys sitting beside her when you are hitting her like that?" she reasoned with them.

However, the boys were not going down without a battle. If they were going to be taken away, they were going out kicking and screaming. Davey grabbed at anything he could find to help hold his place at the table. The only thing he could grasp that was tangible was his glass of milk. With all the flailing body parts, Mary knew the milk would not fair well. Her goal was to reach over and take it from him before it spilled. But almost as soon as she did, a stray kick made contact with her hand, and the glass of milk emptied its contents directly in her lap.

As soon as the cold milk hit, a scream erupted from the startled grandmother. The commotion immediately stopped, and the room became extremely quiet. All eyes were on Mary, who had a stray drop of milk slowly carousing down through her bangs and across her forehead.

"Now look what your fighting has done, boys," Max said, clearly disappointed with the behavior of his twin sons.

The boys both teared up immediately. They hadn't meant for this to happen to their grandmother. This was just another accident. They loved Grandma Mary, and had fought for her attention. And now she was covered with their spilled milk.

There was a moment of uncomfortable silence, and then Grandpa Joseph sprang into action and grabbed a dish towel from the kitchen to wipe up his soggy wife. Angel and Max removed the boys from the table. As they headed to the living room for a time-out on the couch, Grandma Mary could hear their tearful pleas.

"It was an accident," Johnny called over his father's shoulder, choking up as he fought back the tears threatening to spill out.

"Yeah! It wasn't supposed to happen," Davey agreed from his place in his mother's arms.

Mary felt defeated and, for a moment, she let her head rest in her hands. Joseph continued his efforts to dry his soggy wife off, and then gently asked if she was okay.

"I'm fine," she reassured him. "Just a little wet and feeling like a kid who just lost the milking contest at the county fair!"

She glanced at her watch, and then added, "We need to think about leaving anyway. Let me go change my clothes so we can get ready to head out."

Before exiting the room, she turned back to her husband and smiled when she realized he was cleaning off the table. Why did it take a calamity to get him to help out with the housework?

Calling back to him, she said, "All is not lost, you know. It appears the boys have learned the meaning of 'accident.' Now we need to work on securing their surroundings to keep the accidents from happening to begin with!"

She returned a short time later, dressed in a fresh outfit with her hair sporting a blown-dried look. Both boys greeted her with a hug, followed by an apology. She returned the hugs, kissed each head, and reassured them that accidents do happen. *And frequently, with boys like you*, she thought to herself.

"So, let's head to the church so we can get Davey ready to be a shepherd boy," Grandma Mary said with a smile.

****

A short time later, they arrived at the church and stepped into a flurry of activity. The basement was full of costumes, children, and adults who were fussing over the children. The church's live nativity was always a highlight of the Christmas season for Angel's family.

They quickly located an outfit for Davey and set about transforming him into a shepherd boy from centuries past. At first, Johnny was caught up in the excitement of all the activity around him. But when he saw that most of the attention was focused on Davey, it became his goal to change that.

"I'm hungry," he complained.

"You're not hungry, Johnny," his mother reassured him. "We just ate."

"But you didn't let me finish my supper," he argued. When that failed to gain a response, he tried another approach. "I'm thirsty then."

Angel and Grandma Mary paused and looked at each other for a brief moment. After looking around the busy room, Mary told her daughter, "It's too much work to get to the kitchen for a glass of water."

Angel nodded her head in agreement and said, "It won't hurt him to wait. Plus, if we give him something to drink, then he will complain that he has to go to the bathroom."

When Johnny saw that his efforts were fruitless, he said, "It's too noisy in here. I'm getting a headache."

Davey looked at his brother and said, "Stop whining, Johnny. You're just jealous that I'm gonna be in the play and you aren't."

"No way!" Johnny insisted. "I don't want to be in the stupid play! And anyway, you look like a girl in that dress!"

"It's not a dress!" Davey yelled back. "It's a shepherd's outfit!" Davey picked up his staff, as if he intended to hit his brother with it, but Angel stepped in between them.

Seeing the unwanted attention from the other participants focusing on them, Angel decided something needed to be done with Johnny. She looked at her mother and said, "I hate to ask, but can you finish helping Davey with his costume while I take Johnny to join his father and Grandpa Joseph?"

Mary reassured her daughter that she did not mind

in the least. As Angel and Johnny departed, Grandma Mary returned to the task of fitting Davey's costume. She had just finished tying the band around his head when Margaret Wellington chose to grace them with her presence. Looking up from her kneeling position, Mary accidentally let a groan slip out.

"Are you okay, Mary?" Margaret inquired.

Recovering quickly, Mary pushed herself off the floor into an upright position and cheerfully replied, "Everything's fine, Margaret. It's just not as easy to get up as it used to be."

Turning her attention to Davey, Margaret said, "What a nice looking shepherd boy. Is this one of your grandchildren?"

"It sure is," Mary proudly replied, patting Davey on the head. "This is one of Angel's twins."

"Well, he certainly is a good-looking young man," Margaret smiled down at him.

Margaret's positive mannerism caught Mary off-guard, and she wasn't quite sure what to say next. But the glory of the moment was short-lived, with Margaret's next actions bringing her crashing back to earth.

Reaching over, Margaret gave Davey's outfit a little tweak. "Let's just adjust your headpiece a bit. Your grandmother didn't put it on straight, and you don't want to look silly wearing a crooked headpiece."

Mary's eyes narrowed as she watched Margaret Wellington make an almost imaginary adjustment to Davey's costume. The gesture had clearly been intended only as an insult to her.

Mary could feel her blood pressure begin to rise. Margaret could insult her in front of her adult children, because they could see right through her, but she was not going to get away with making her look bad in front of her grandchildren!

At that moment, Angel returned from her mission of dropping Johnny off. She wasn't sure what had just happened, but she could sense the tension between the two ladies in front of her.

"Is everything okay?" she asked, trying to sound

cheerful and light-hearted.

Mary pointed an accusing finger at Margaret and said loudly, "She..." Quickly realizing how immature an approach that was, she regrouped and said, "It..."

Poor, innocent Mary didn't realize how badly her choice of words sounded together until there was a collective gasp and the room grew silent. She looked around and all eyes were focused on her. It was then that she realized "she" and "it" were two one-syllable words that should never be uttered together, especially in the church fellowship hall, which was currently full of church members busily preparing for one of the holiest events of the year.

Quick to defend herself, Mary called out, "That wasn't a swear word."

Davey reached over and tugged on her sleeve. "It sounded like one to me, Grandma," he innocently stated.

"No," Mary insisted again. "I didn't swear. It was just a very poor choice of one syllable words."

Fortunately, most members decided they had too much to do to worry about whether Mary Davis had just sworn in the church fellowship hall or not. They returned to their busy tasks of donning costumes and making final touches for the live nativity.

Margaret Wellington, always anxious to have the last say and appear the victor in any situation, simply stated, "Whatever!" and marched off to find some task that needed her attention.

Mary could only stand there, as if frozen in time, red-faced and embarrassed to the core. Margaret had once again managed to coerce her into making a fool of herself. She wanted to just sit down and cry.

Realizing her mother's discomfort, Angel said, "Mom, why don't you go help Dad and Max with Johnny. He's probably driving them both nuts by now anyway."

Mary decided some fresh air would be good for her right now, so she took Angel's advice and numbly made her way outside to find the other half of Angel's family.

******

One look at Mary, and Joseph knew something was just not right.

"Is everything okay?" he questioned.

What had just transpired in the church basement was nothing Mary wanted to relive. She would share her frustration and embarrassment with Joseph in the privacy of their home, but this was not the place and time to discuss it. So she simply nodded her head and found a seat beside them. Angel joined them a short time later, and the nativity scene began to come to life, one participant at a time.

The shepherd boys came in shortly thereafter, led by a cluster of glittery angels. Next came the noble and elegant Wise Men, carrying their gifts of gold, frankincense, and myrrh. Lastly, came the two older children who portrayed Mary and Joseph. Mary carried a lively, little baby Jesus, who was kicking and cooing all the way.

As Davey walked past his family, he smiled and waved freely, temporarily forgetting that he was a shepherd boy in search of a newborn Savior. Angel and Mary smiled and waved back, while Johnny crossed his eyes and stuck his tongue out at him.

The live nativity seemed to be going well, and Mary began to relax, letting the stress of her last interaction with Margaret Wellington fade into the recesses of her mind. Davey seated himself on a bale of hay and watched the activity around him.

Angel watched her youngest son for a moment, and then looked nervously at her mother.

"I hope he behaves himself," she whispered. "As you may be aware, my sons can quite frequently embarrass me in public settings."

Mary reached over and took her daughter's hand. Giving it a gentle squeeze, she said, "He'll do just fine, sweetie.

He just needs to sit still and look cute.”

“Oh, the cute part is not a problem,” Angel smiled back. “It’s the sitting still piece that worries me.”

And sure enough, it wasn’t long before Davey started getting restless. But it didn’t appear to be related to boredom. It looked more like a discomfort issue. He kept rubbing his eyes and wiping at his nose. Then he would throw a look of distress his mother’s way.

Before Angel made the connection, Davey began to sneeze. He sneezed over and over again. It was Max who figured out what the problem was.

“He’s sitting on a bale of hay,” he whispered to his wife. “Hay must trigger his allergies, just like it does with me.”

“Yes,” Angel agreed, “I think you are right. I didn’t think about the hay.”

The family watched helplessly as Davey’s sneezes became more frequent and more violent.

“Do something for him, Mommy!” Johnny demanded.

But Angel wasn’t sure exactly what she could do. If she went to help him, it would be a distraction to the whole live nativity scene. But eyes were beginning to focus his way, as others became aware of his dilemma.

Johnny finally decided someone needed to take action. Davey needed help, and if Mom and Dad weren’t going to do something, he would have to.

“He needs some of Daddy’s medicine!” Johnny said loudly.

“Shhh!” Angel tried to silence him. It was true that Davey had inherited his allergies from his father, but medicine wouldn’t solve the immediate dilemma.

Being quieted by his mother only frustrated Johnny further. So, Johnny took matters into his own hands. Looking Davey’s way, he called out, “Davey, want some of Daddy’s medicine?”

Davey looked his way, while all four adults tried to quiet Johnny down. But Johnny would have none of it. Ignoring their request to settle down, he defiantly called out, “Want some of Daddy's Viagra?!"

Some of the congregants chuckled, some gasped, while others just looked their way in a stunned silence. Angel hung her head and covered her face with her hands. Max stood up and reached past his wife and mother-in-law to try to contain his wayward son's behavior.

As he bent down to pick Johnny up, the man sitting next to them said, "Viagra, huh?!"

Max picked up Johnny, and choosing not to make eye contact, simply replied, "I assure you that I do not take Viagra for my allergies!"

Mary put a reassuring arm around her humiliated daughter. Then she whispered words of assurance in her ear.

"As I told Gloria on her day, the things that humiliate us the most often make the funniest memories."

"I sure hope so," Angel replied through the hands which still covered her face, "because this sure is humiliating!"

****

****

Berry

****

Chapter 11
Berry

✼✼✼✼✼✼✼

Mary awoke with a smile on her face. She knew it wasn't fair to laugh at the discomfort and embarrassment Johnny had caused his father at the nativity scene the night before. Yet, it felt good that it had been someone else, other than herself, that had been the focus of the embarrassment. She had taken center stage in the play of humility far too many times in the last few days.

Remembering that this was Berry's day to visit, Mary's smile abruptly faded. A look of terror took its place. This was the day she had dreaded – skiing at Dorr Mountain.

Berry had always loved the great outdoors. During the summertime, he would stay outside until it was dark, and his mother had forced him to come inside. Even in the cold of the winter, he loved to spend time outside, filling his free time with sledding, skiing or just building snow forts.

So Mary and Joseph were not surprised when he acquired a management position at Dorr Mountain Ski Area in the neighboring town of Mendon. It was a position he fit into naturally, and he put his whole heart into it. His wife, Olivia, complimented him in his role there. She was just as actively involved, providing ski lessons, and helping to organize special events.

Berry had invited his parents to come visit his ski area several times, but to no avail. In their retirement, they hadn't seemed interested in sharing his love for the great outdoors. But today was different. It was his day to have his parent's undivided attention, and he was intent on showing off his home turf. This wasn't just his job - it was his life.

Berry knew his parents hadn't skied for years, but he would make it easy for them. They would start on the beginner's slope and see how well they managed there. They could keep it simple, if need be. And if they ran into any problems, both he and Olivia would be right there to help them out. What could possibly go wrong?

So with the plans made for the day, Berry and Olivia arrived on Day Ten, bearing gifts of freshly-made doughnuts and coffee lattes. At the front door of the Davis homestead, Berry paused to smile at the holly berries adorning the main entrance.

"That is cute, Mom," he said aloud, juggling the box of doughnuts in one hand while trying to open the door with the other.

Mary and Joseph had not attempted to ski for more years than they wanted to think about. But at Berry's persistent request, they had finally relented and decided to give it a whirl. With twelve kids who had participated in outdoor winter sports throughout their childhood, they had enough leftover equipment in the basement to start their own secondhand shop. Mary had done some exploring and found ski outfits complete with boots, poles and skiis that would work for both Joseph and herself. She had everything laid out in the entry way awaiting Berry's arrival.

After the initial greetings, Berry looked around and said, "I see you found some old equipment."

Mary chuckled and said, "With leftovers from twelve kids, we probably have more than we need."

Olivia had been looking over the skiing equipment and seemed concerned about the age. "We have newer equipment that you can use," she suggested.

Mary looked anxiously at Joseph, and then cautiously replied, "I think we will be okay with this stuff, don't you? It hasn't been that long since they have been used."

Berry spoke up and said, "But this equipment is a little old and might be brittle. You would be much better off using our rental ones."

Joseph merely shrugged. Skiing was definitely not his specialty. He had skied frequently as a teenager, but that was decades ago. Their equipment was probably a bit outdated and old-fashioned, but this was only going to be a one-day event. And who knew how long they would ski. If his back gave out, or it proved too strenuous for their aging bodies, one trip down the mountainside might be all they would (or could) do. After thinking it through for a moment, he agreed with his wife.

"I think we will be okay. And if not, we can always check out your rental equipment when we get there," he said.

Berry was not convinced that their equipment was okay, but hoped he could talk them into renting some once they reached the ski area. As the manager of such a facility, he knew the risks of using outdated equipment. Yet, on the other hand, as the son of Mary Davis, he also knew how challenging it could be to win an argument.

He decided to let the topic go for now. Who knew if they would actually make it onto the mountain anyway. They might find that Mary and Joseph were too uncomfortable or awkward on the skiis, and might not want to try a trip down the slope. If that became the case, they would just hang out at the lodge and Berry would show them around.

With the equipment issue resolved for the moment, the four adults had a quick breakfast of fresh doughnuts and finished off their lattes. Then they adorned their ski outfits and headed to check out Berry's ski resort.

****

Once at Dorr Mountain, Mary and Joseph strapped on their skiis while Berry and Olivia gave them a refresher course. They did a trial run down the beginner slope, and both of the older adults did remarkably well. Mary was extremely pleased at the way she handled her skiis, and felt ready to take on the world. Joseph felt he had done well, too, so they decided to take a trip up the ski lift.

Before heading for the lift, Berry once again cautiously

approached the topic of renting equipment. But as he expected, he was met with resistance from his mother.

"We will probably only take one trip down the mountain, sweetie," she insisted. "There's no point in wasting time getting fitted for equipment when we already have everything we need right here."

Berry shot his father a concerned look. Joseph only raised an eyebrow and shrugged a shoulder. He had also learned through past experience that it could be difficult to win an argument with a woman who had already made up her mind.

So they proceeded to the chairlift, and Berry instructed his parents on how to properly enter and exit the lift. He told his parents to just watch them if they had any questions. Berry and Olivia had been on and off the chairlift so many times, they could do it with their eyes closed.

With that, the younger couple hopped onto the chairlift and then watched anxiously over their shoulders to make sure Mary and Joseph were successfully seated themselves. All went well, and Mary gave her son a "thumbs up" to indicate things were fine.

Berry turned to face forward and said to his wife, "I knew this would be good for them. I just wanted to get them out of the house and into the great outdoors."

Olivia looked backward to smile and wave at her in-laws, then turned to her husband and said, "So far, so good, but we haven't made it the base of the mountain yet. A lot can happen between now and then."

"I know," Berry agreed, pausing for a moment to contemplate everything that might go wrong. "And they haven't got very good equipment."

"That is quite true," Olivia agreed. Then seeing the look of concern on her husband's face, she added, "But we will be right there with them."

"And Mom said it's only one trip, right?" he added, trying to maintain his mother's positive attitude.

Olivia cautiously nodded, and then turned to face her

husband. "I hope we are doing the right thing and not pushing them too far."

Berry smiled, and reached over to give his wife a hug. "One thing you need to remember about my parents is that they are very resilient. We will get through this."

He glanced back over his shoulder to see how his parents were doing. All looked well, so he gave them a thumb's up. Turning back to his wife, he added, "One way or another!"

Mary had done well up until this point, but once they were on the chairlift, her confidence started to fade.

"What are we doing, Joseph?" she asked her husband nervously.

Joseph felt a bit edgy himself, but he didn't want to impose his concerns on his wife's already weakening resolve. So he put an arm around her shoulder and stated, "We are going skiing with our son and his wife, and we are going to have a great time!"

"I like your optimism, Joseph," Mary replied, "but I can't guarantee that it what will happen."

Mary looked over her shoulder and down at the trail beneath them and said, "It sure is a long way down to the bottom of this hill….and the higher we go, the more nervous I seem to be getting."

Joseph knew if his wife could just relax, things would go much better. He didn't want her to get so stressed out that she couldn't enjoy herself, so he came up with an idea to try to help. He would give Mary a bit of her own philosophy and help her to focus on the positive.

"Mary," he said calmly, giving her shoulder a little squeeze. "It is a beautiful day out here. The sun is shining, there is blue sky above us, and we are having a great time with our son, Berry, and his wife. So why don't you just close your eyes, breathe deeply, and relax. Looking around might only make you more nervous."

Joseph's plan sounded good to Mary, so she settled back, closed her eyes and took a deep breath of fresh, cool mountain air. After a moment or two, Mary actually found herself quite relaxed. Joseph was right, as usual. They would have a good day with Berry and Olivia. They were a privileged couple, to be able to ski at the facility their son managed. And although they hadn't skied for years, it was a skill that you don't forget - like walking, or talking, or riding a bike, just like Joy had suggested.

Mary talked herself right into making the most of the day and became so relaxed, she failed to hear her husband warn her that it was time to dismount from the chairlift. By the time she realized what was happening, it was too late to react. Joseph was gone, and Mary was not prepared to follow him. She watched over her shoulder in total despair as the distance between them grew.

Joseph stood on the platform watching as well. He seemed frozen in time, unable to take his eyes off her as she drifted away. But Berry came over and broke the spell.

"Where's mom?" he asked.

Joseph could only manage to point up the hill, and Berry turned to see his mother, still in the chairlift, heading further up the mountain.

"She didn't get off?" asked Olivia, coming up behind them.

Joseph watched his wife grow smaller by the second, and could only shake his head in the negative. He knew how nervous Mary had been while he still sat beside her, so she must be terrified now that she was alone - and heading to higher ground. Finally, he found his voice.

"She'll kill herself if she skiis from the top of the mountain," he stated flatly.

Mary realized facing backward would not help her now. Her family had turned into tiny, little people beneath her on the landing platform, and they were not going to be able to help her now. She closed her eyes for a moment, in an effort to collect her thoughts, and also try to slow the panic that was welling up inside of her.

However, it didn't work. Her eyes immediately flew

open wide, and she called out to no one in particular, "I'll kill myself if I ski from the top of the mountain!"

She knew there was no going back, but she also knew she couldn't go forward. And the longer she waited, the further she was from where she wanted to be - at the foot of the mountain. The bar of the chairlift was still in the upright position, where Joseph had left it when he exited. Mary looked at the ground and decided it didn't look too far down. She would simply jump, that's all. It would be the quickest and most direct route to where she wanted to be – on the ground.

She didn't hesitate, knowing if she did, her courage would leave her. So she slid to the edge of the chairlift, closed her eyes and leapt out of her seat. She felt herself falling through the frozen air and knew it probably wasn't going to feel good when she met up with the packed snow beneath her.

All too soon, she crashed to the snow-covered earth below. She heard a crack and waited to feel the pain. Something inside her told her this was not good. With a snap that loud, it had to have been a major bone breaking.

Mary lay on the frozen ground, not daring to move for fear of dislocating the broken limb. But, after what seemed like just short of forever, the anticipated pain failed to materialize. So she slowly pulled herself into a sitting position to investigate the source of the crack.

She was immediately relieved to see that it was her ski that had snapped in two, not her leg. However, as she contemplated the situation, her relief began to turn to panic. How could she possibly get down the mountain with a broken ski?

Mary wrestled her way to her feet and stood looking helplessly at her V-shaped ski. If she was a woman who was known to swear, she would have used those two one syllable words "she" and "it" right now. But she immediately pushed the thought from her mind. Mary had never found that foul language solved any problems, and she didn't see how it would help her now.

Berry had been right. They shouldn't have used the old, brittle equipment. But who would have known it could come to this, with her jumping off the chairlift? Mary wanted to cry, but what good would that do? Beating herself up for using old equipment, or sitting down and crying, would be just about as useless as the cursing would be. What she needed right now was some help.

She began to scour the mountainside. Surely there would be someone there who could help her. But, her heart sunk when she failed to spot another living soul. It was like she was totally abandoned on top of this God-forsaken mountain. She had been nervous about the skiing plans right from the start. Why hadn't she just put her foot down and simply said "No?!" They could have gone bowling, or out to a movie, or something that would not have left her in a crazy predicament like this.

Stop it, Mary, she said to herself. *Just pull yourself together and think.*

She paused to weigh her options. She could just stay where she was and wait for help to arrive. Somebody would come along eventually. Or, she could take her skiis off altogether and walk down the mountain.

Mary turned to look down the mountain and, realizing how far it was to the base, she opted for the first choice. She would just sit and wait. So she sat down on the frozen tundra and waited. But, as she sat there, a cool breeze began to blow.

Mary had never really enjoyed the coldness of winter. When the kids had gone outside to play, she had always stayed inside and made hot chocolate and cookies to greet them when they returned. She quickly realized sitting still was not going to work for her. She decided the sooner she could get off that crazy mountain, the better she would feel.

She stood up and bent down to check out her ski. Maybe she could straighten it out, or pop it back together. Maybe if she was lucky, she could find a way to make it flat enough to function and get her down the mountain. If not, she would just take them off and start walking.

However, luck had never been a friend of Mary's. As she bent over to work on her ski, she slowly started to slide down the mountain - and backwards at that. Looking out of the corner of her eye, Mary suddenly realized that she was in motion. She managed to grab her ski poles before they were out of reach, but she was already picking up momentum and found she was unable to stop herself.

"No!! Help me!!" she screamed to nobody in particular, since she appeared to be completely alone.

"Stop!" she yelled, looking down at her skiis as if they were human and could obey her command.

She tried to dig her poles into the packed snow that surrounded her, but they failed to grip and did nothing more than drag along behind her, leaving a trail that spelled out Mary's horror and despair.

Realizing there was little that she could do to help herself, she instead decided to do all she could to protect herself. She crouched down into a ball, assuming a fetal position on her skiis, and waited for the crash.

This isn't going to be pretty, she thought to herself. Then she called up into the cold, winter sky and said, "God, don't let me die. I only have a few more days to get through, and Joy needs me for the tree lighting!"

****

Meanwhile, Joseph, Berry, and Olivia had been frantically trying to figure out the best way to reach Mary. They had decided Joseph should ski down the mountain and wait for her at the base, in the event that she should surprise them all and make it down on her own. Olivia would take the chairlift to the top of the mountain and ski the full length of the trail to try to spot her. And Berry would go get some help from Ski Patrol.

Joseph skied like the wind and made it to the base

in no time. He wasn't sure if it was because he retained his skiing skills and abilities from years gone by or, more likely, if it was just fear and adrenalin pumping through his veins. His goal was to reach the bottom as fast as he could so he could scour the trail upward for his lost wife.

After an eternity of waiting, or so it seemed to Joseph, he spotted Olivia coming down the trail. He stared profusely against the bright white glare of the snow, but his heart sunk when he realized she was alone. She apparently hadn't found Mary. She skied up beside Joseph and slid to a stop.

"No sign of her?" Joseph queried, sounding completely dismayed.

Olivia pulled her goggles off and shook her head sadly. "Nothing," she stated. "I looked for her all the way down, but didn't see any sign anywhere."

"Where could she be?" Joseph asked nervously. "How could she have disappeared?"

Olivia put an arm around his waist to reassure him, although she was feeling apprehensive herself. Skiing was an awesome thrill, but she knew how dangerous it could be. Maybe bringing her in-laws here for the day had not been such a good idea. But she had to remain positive, for the sake of her father-in-law.

"Well, we know what trail she is on, so it shouldn't be too hard to find her," she tried her best to reassure him.

Joseph looked at her anxiously, not convinced that this day would have a happy ending.

Olivia gently rubbed his back and tried to sound casual. "Don't worry, Dad. Berry knows this mountain like the back of his hand," she said calmly.

She paused for a moment, not sure what to do next. Then, deciding that standing in the cold staring up the mountainside trail wasn't really solving anything, she suggested, "Why don't we go into the lodge so I can check with the staff and see if Berry has made any progress finding her. We'll get you a cup of coffee and try to figure out what to do next."

Joseph smiled half-heartedly and said, "If I was prone to drinking, I would probably want something stronger than coffee right now."

Olivia smiled and led Joseph toward the lodge. It resembled guiding a robot, or walking a zombie. Joseph was almost paralyzed with fear for Mary's safety, and Olivia began to worry about him, too.

They stepped into the warmth of the base lodge and were greeted by the noisy hustle and bustle of the indoor activities. A large fire roared in the oversized stone fireplace, located in the center of the room. Some skiers scurried about, as if in a hurry to don their gear and hit the trails, while others relaxed casually on the sofas, probably resting from their last run down the mountainside.

In one corner of the room was a table sporting a massive gingerbread house, which was being raffled to raise funds for Project CARE. And who should be standing behind the table, obviously in charge of the event, was none other than Margaret Wellington.

Joseph had not ventured very far into the room, still appearing to be numb and unaware of his surroundings. However, the moment he focused on the likes of Margaret Wellington, he bounced back to life and immediately turned to head for the exit. He had enough to worry about right now, and he didn't need to deal with whatever she was up to as well.

But it was too late. Margaret had already spotted him and was heading his way. She proved to be faster than he was. Still in his state of confusion, she quickly overtook him before he was able to reach the door.

"Joey, what a pleasant surprise," she said, in her sickeningly sweet voice.

Maybe for you, Joseph thought to himself. But more politely, he turned to face her and said, "Nice to see you, Margaret."

Olivia had gone to get Joseph a cup of coffee and returned just at that moment. She had never had the "pleasure" of meeting Margaret Wellington before, but had heard the stories that had floated through her in-law's family. She handed the cup of coffee to Joseph while he made introductions, and she politely shook Margaret's hand.

Margaret returned her attention to Joseph and said, "You look terrible, Joseph." A look of concern crossed her face before she asked, "Whatever is the matter?"

Joseph explained how Mary was lost on the mountain. He knew deep inside himself that the less he told Margaret Wellington, the better off they would all be. But, she looked genuinely concerned and once he opened his mouth, he just couldn't seem to stop himself.

He told her how they should have rented newer equipment, and how Mary had been nervous on the chairlift. How he had told her to close her eyes and relax, but then she had forgotten to get off the chairlift. Now she was lost on the mountain, and it was all his fault.

Margaret patted him sympathetically on the shoulder and reassured him that it was not his fault. She led him over to one of the sofas in front of the fire and encouraged him to sit down. And then, of course, she seated herself cozily beside him, completely forgetting the task of managing her fundraising booth and guarding the giant gingerbread house. Olivia followed along and settled on the sofa on the opposite side of Joseph.

Sitting in front of the fire with what seemed like empathetic beings on either side, Joseph's heart started to melt. He feared he would break down and cry. Olivia was rubbing his back and Margaret seemed to truly care about Mary's safe return. But, the next icy words that protruded from Margaret's mouth suddenly jolted him back to reality.

"You can't blame yourself, Joey," she reassured him. "That woman just has a knack for getting herself into predicaments!"

Joseph's head shot up and he stared coldly at Margaret. Who was she to criticize Mary? At least Mary had a heart of gold and everything she did in life was out of an act of love.

Margaret Wellington couldn't get past loving the person in the mirror. Her priorities in life only revolved around making the reflection in her mirror happy.

Joseph could think of a hundred things to say to Margaret Wellington at this moment, but none of them were nice, and none of them came close to being polite.

At that precise moment, the front door of the lodge opened and in walked Berry, with an arm around his very distraught mother. Poor Mary looked like she had been through a hurricane. Her hair stuck out wildly everywhere, with little branches and twigs caught in it. Her face was scratched, and she had a tear in her snowsuit that left the inner lining hanging out.

Joseph and Olivia jumped up and rushed over to greet the pair, both questioning if she was alright, if anything was broken, and wanting to know what had happened. The trio escorted her over to the sofa and Margaret got up so Mary could have a seat.

Margaret never said a word, not even voicing concern about Mary's well-being. She simply stood there and observed, a blank expression covering her face. The concern of the family members over their mother and wife was quite obvious.

Mary stiffly lowered herself onto the awaiting couch. She didn't think she had broken anything, but now that the adrenalin was starting to wane, she could feel some aches and pains.

Once Mary seemed settled, Berry recanted the tale of how he went with the Ski Patrol to find her. Fortunately, she had worn a brightly colored jacket. Otherwise, they might not have found her so quickly.

After Mary had started sliding backwards down the hillside, her skiis had apparently turned, possibly because one was broken. So instead of going straight down the hill, she had cut diagonally across the trail and directly into the brush located on the side of the trail. So she hadn't slid too far, or built up enough momentum, to cause serious bodily harm. But, it was enough speed to thrust her into the brush, where she became hopelessly entangled and was having a great deal of difficulty freeing herself.

Joseph sat on the couch beside his distraught wife and pulled her close to comfort her. Seeing this, Margaret Wellington excused herself, stating she needed to return to her table to try to raise funds to support the needy families of Project CARE. She walked away while Berry and Olivia pulled chairs over to sit closer to the elder adults.

Mary wanted to cry, but there was no way she was going to fall apart with Margaret Wellington in the room. She looked at the faces of her loved ones around her and knew she had to lighten up – for their sakes, anyway.

"Well, at least I made it off the mountain with no broken bones," she stated flatly.

"And it looks like you brought some of the mountain with you," Olivia said light-heartedly. She reached over and gently pulled a twig out of her mother-in-law's frazzled hair.

"Look! A souvenir!" Berry said cheerfully, taking the twig from his wife and handing it to his mother. "Now you have something to remind you of your skiing adventure on Dorr Mountain."

Mary smiled weakly, not quite ready to make light of the situation. The trauma of it all was still too fresh in her mind.

So Berry came up with another plan. "Here," he said, standing up. "Let me go buy you a ticket to the gingerbread house raffle. Maybe you will win, and that will cheer you up."

"Don't waste your money," Mary warned him. "I am not a lucky winner. You could buy every ticket but the last one, and I still wouldn't win."

"What are you talking about?" Joseph prodded her. "You got me, didn't you? That was pretty lucky!"

Mary smiled at her husband, while her son and daughter-in-law joined in.

"Yeah! And you've got us, too!" they smiled at her.

Mary leaned against her husband and said, "In that area, I am indeed a very fortunate woman. I have been blessed with the best family in the world!"

Berry stood up, kissed his mother on the head, and said, "And now, I am going to buy that winning ticket for you!"

He returned a few minutes later, stating Margaret was going to announce the winner in about thirty minutes.

"Why don't we just go over to the café and get a bite to eat?" Berry suggested, pointing to the small café in the corner.

"It's a waste of time to wait," Mary reiterated, "but I am famished and would love a bite to eat."

Putting an arm around his mother's waist as she stood to her feet, Berry teased her. "Clawing your way out of the brush is a lot of work, isn't it?!"

Mary gave her son a playful slap on the shoulder and said, "You be nice to your mother. She has had a rough morning."

The two couples seated themselves at a table in the café and ordered some lunch. Soon they were laughing and joking about Mary's flight off the chairlift, her newly designed V-shaped skiis, and her nap in the bushes.

"Now do you see why I didn't want you to use outdated equipment?" Berry questioned, looking directly at his mother. "You probably would have made it safely off the mountain if your equipment had been newer."

The group waited with baited breath, not sure how Mary would respond to her son's challenging words. But, she simply donned an offended look and replied, "But I did make it safely off the mountain, Berry."

Berry smiled and said, "I meant standing in an upright position on your skiis, not rolling down the slope!"

Olivia thought for a moment, and then added, "Just think how big a snowball you could have made before you reached the base!"

The two couples paused to envision Mary rolling down the mountainside as a giant snowball, limbs sticking out and a frazzled expression on her face. As they did, they simultaneously burst into a round of hilarious laughter.

The group was having such a good time making light of

Mary's mishap, that they didn't realize a half hour had already passed. The four of them looked up in surprise when Margaret Wellington approached their table.

She looked dolefully at Mary and said, "You have won the gingerbread house." It was almost as if she dreaded to give her the good news.

"No way," Mary argued. "I've never won anything in my life!"

"Seriously?!" Berry asked, looking up at Margaret for confirmation.

The look on Margaret's face was confirmation enough. She clearly had not wanted Mary to win, but it was her Christian duty to do the right thing. And Mary's name was the one written on the winning ticket that had been pulled from the jar.

Mary let out a whoop and, temporarily forgetting her freshly acquired aches and pains, jumped up to go claim her prize. She took a few steps, but then stopped and turned around.

"With the kind of day I've been having," she began, "I think someone else should carry it for me."

"Good idea," Joseph agreed.

"Let's have Berry carry it," Olivia suggested.

Mary and Berry proudly went to retrieve the prize. Mary's face beamed as she returned to the café table with her newly acquired prize possession. The rest of the lunch was a mixture of laughter and fun, the trials of the morning forgotten with the winning of the gingerbread house. After finishing up their lunch, the younger couple decided it was a good time to head home to a safer environment for their weary parents.

****

The two couples arrived back at the Davis homestead and were promptly greeted by Buzzy in the front yard.

"Buzzy is still around?" Berry asked. It seemed like

that dog must have already lived two life spans.

"Who's Buzzy?" Olivia asked.

As they were getting out of the car, Berry explained to his wife that Buzzy was the neighborhood dog who belonged to no one, yet everyone.

Mary went to retrieve her gingerbread house from the back of the car, but then thought better of it.

"You did a good job carrying it at the resort," she said to Berry, "Why don't you carry it into the house. With my luck, I would probably trip over Buzzy or a crack in the sidewalk."

"You were lucky enough to win it," Olivia reminded her mother-in-law.

"Much to Margaret Wellington's dismay," smirked Berry.

Berry walked to the rear of the car and carefully picked up the gingerbread house. Mary rushed ahead of him to unlock and open the front door, but a commotion behind her caught her attention. Buzzy appeared to be in attack mode, and was currently heading Berry's way.

"What is wrong with you, Buzzy?" Joseph questioned him.

"Buzzy, stop!" Mary scolded him. "You know who Berry is."

But Buzzy would have none of it. He was not happy about something and Berry seemed to be his closest target. Being quick-witted, Mary summed up the situation and came to the conclusion that it was their winter outfits Buzzy did not approve of.

"These are not uniforms, Buzzy!" Mary called uselessly to him. "This is outdoor snow gear."

Whatever it was seemed to matter little to Buzzy. He didn't like it, and he wasn't going to let anyone get away with wearing an unusual outfit like that in his neighborhood.

Berry tried to slip past Buzzy and make a run for the door, but Buzzy was smaller and faster. He grabbed one of Berry's pant legs and began to shake it ferociously. It proved to be powerful enough to throw Berry off balance and the remaining three adults watched in horror as Mary's beautiful prize gingerbread house came crashing down on the sidewalk and landed in a massive heap.

As if realizing he had just created a disaster, and wanting nothing to do with it, Buzzy released Berry's pant leg and promptly left the yard. All four adults stood momentarily frozen in time, staring intensely at the pile of crumpled gingerbread house on the ground. Then three pair of eyes looked up at a disheartened Mary, who simply stood there, unable to speak and once more looking close to tears.

Olivia was the first to react.

"I'm going to take Mom inside and make her a cup of hot tea," she announced.

"Good idea," Berry agreed.

"We'll clean this up and be in shortly," Joseph added.

Olivia escorted her mother-in-law into the house, settled her at the kitchen counter, and put a kettle of water on to heat. While they waited for the tea kettle to whistle, Mary shared some of her sorrows with Olivia.

"Life is so hard to understand," she began. "With all that I do right, it's hard to comprehend why so much goes wrong."

"I know," Olivia said, sympathetically, rubbing her mother-in-law's back. "You try so hard, but sometimes things just don't work out right."

"Sometimes?" Mary questioned. "In my life, things rarely work out right."

"Don't be so hard on yourself," Olivia reassured her. "You did a great job raising your family. You have twelve wonderful kids and an awesome husband."

"Yes, I suppose that is all true," Mary agreed, and then continued, "but I will admit it did really bother me to finally make it to the base of the mountain, only to find my husband sitting cozily on the sofa in the lodge beside old, mean Margaret Wellington."

"Oh, no," Olivia shook her head emphatically. "That was not what it appeared. Dad was trying to get away from her. He was so worried about you that he didn't know what to do with himself. I went to get him a cup of coffee. He sat down to drink it, and she sat right on the sofa beside him. But their whole conversation was about you.”

“There was nothing more to it than that?” Mary asked, looking over her shoulder at her daughter-in-law.

“Mom, I don’t think you need to worry about Margaret Wellington,” Olivia insisted. “Why would Dad want an ice queen like her when he has a wonderful, warm-hearted wife like you?”

“Thank you, sweetie,” Mary said softly, reaching over to pat Olivia’s hand.

At that moment, the men came into the kitchen carrying what was left of the gingerbread house. It was a sorry sight, nothing but broken pieces and tiny reminders of the beautiful structure it once was.

“Sorry, Mom,” Berry apologized. “Buzzy was not kind to your gingerbread house.”

“It doesn’t matter, honey,” Mary said, smiling up at him.

“But it kind of ruined your day,” Berry said sadly. “I was hoping it would end on a happy note.”

“Oh, but it was a good day,” Mary insisted, and then added, “in between catastrophes, anyway!”

Olivia had finished making a cup of tea for Mary and leaned over the counter to set it in front of her. Without a moment’s hesitation, Mary picked up a piece of the gingerbread house and took a bite of it.

“We can still eat it,” she said through her mouthful.

Berry laughed at his mother and followed suit. He grabbed a piece of it as well and took a bite. “Umm,” he said, then glancing at his father, he added, “You must have just salted the sidewalk, Dad. It tastes a little salty.”

Olivia chuckled and grabbed a piece of her own. “Yum, sweet and salty! Not bad at all!”

“You guys are crazy,” Joseph laughed at them. “Yes, I just salted the sidewalk. And no, I am not eating a piece of sweet and salty gingerbread house!”

“Well, suit yourself,” said Mary, “but we are not going

to let this gingerbread house go to waste. I don't care if it did come from Margaret Wellington, we are going to eat it one way or another."

And just to prove her point, she took another huge bite.

****

✶✶✶✶✶✶✶

Star

✶✶✶✶✶✶✶

Chapter 12
Star

★★★★★★★

Mary awoke with a start. She had been dreaming about being hopelessly lost on a cold, snowy mountaintop. She had been wandering aimlessly all night, alone and destitute. A storm had moved in, and visibly was waning. She was desperate to get off the mountain, but had no idea which way to go. And just when Mary thought things couldn't get worse, she started sliding down the mountain backwards.

Looking at her clock, Mary was relieved to see it was almost time to get up. This was Star's day, and Mary had high hopes for the day ahead of her. Not only was this Day Eleven, and she only have today and tomorrow left to her twelve day plan, but Star was single. Mary truly loved every one of her grandchildren, but it would be a welcome relief to have a quiet day with only adult conversation and activity. And Star had been content with the plan of spending a quiet day at the Davis homestead. This meant Mary and Joseph could sit back and relax, for a change of pace.

Star and her boyfriend, Connor, had flown in yesterday. They had spent the previous night with Connor's parents. Tonight they would stay with Mary and Joseph before heading home tomorrow.

After a quick cup of coffee, Mary hurried to change the scene on the front door to a glittering star. As she decorated the door, she mused about what an appropriate name this had been for her eleventh child. She had always been a quiet, mellow child, but her personality had been as bright as the morning star.

When asked what she wanted to do for the day, Star had simply replied, "Whatever you want, Mom. You are a better planner than I am."

So Mary had opted to just have a quiet day at home, not realizing how much she would appreciate it on day eleven of her twelve day plan. Once the door décor had been adequately converted, she set about preparing a hearty home-cooked meal. Star had always been a thin, underweight child. As an adult, she had not changed. Mary feared that she wasn't eating well, but today would be different. She would make all of Star's favorite dishes, so she wouldn't be able to resist the temptation to eat.

Star had desperately wanted to come home for Thanksgiving, but wanting to accommodate Mary's twelve day plan, and only being able to afford one trip, she had resolved to wait. Mary decided to surprise Star with a second Thanksgiving, complete with all the fixings. She threw a small turkey into the oven and set about making homemade stuffing, sweet potato casserole, and Star's favorite dessert of apple crisp with homemade whipped topping. Today they would lounge around the house, feast on ample portions of food, and watch favorite movies from days gone by.

****

Mary was up to her elbows in flour and food preparation when Star and Connor arrived. She sent Joseph to greet them while she quickly finished the task at hand.

Joseph greeted Star with a big hug. He would agree with his wife that Star had indeed been one of their easier children to raise. He shook hands with Connor and then bent down to retrieve Star's overnight bag.

"Let's get you guys settled in," he said cheerfully. "We are looking forward to a quiet day of table talk and television today. Your mother is in the kitchen preparing a wonderful meal for you right now."

"How has Mom's twelve day plan been going?" Star questioned.

Joseph rolled his eyes and said, "Mom is a little worn out. She's a trooper, as you know, but I think this has been more work than she expected."

Pausing for a moment, Joseph shook Star's bag and said, "You sure travel light."

Star's face immediately grew flushed, and she quickly averted her eyes. But she simply replied, "It was just a quick trip, so we didn't need to bring much with us."

Dad thought nothing more of it, and proceeded to the upper level of the house, where he directed Connor to the room he would be using. Star went to her old bedroom to look around. Seeing not much had changed, she decided she would join her mother in the kitchen to help prepare the meal.

Joseph and Connor returned to the living room and settled down to watch some television. They decided they would utilize this time to watch sports while the ladies were in the kitchen working. Following the meal, the afternoon would be filled with viewing old movies from the stack Mary had left sitting on the coffee table.

Star and her mother had an enjoyable time in the kitchen, peeling potatoes and apples for the meal. While they worked, they caught up on current happenings and laughed about memories from her childhood.

It was proving to be a wonderful day. It was all a Thanksgiving Day should be—food, family and fun conversation. No stress, no trauma, no embarrassing moments. Just family life, simple and at its best.

After a leisurely meal around the table, the four adults cleaned up and gathered in the living room. They let Star choose the first movie, and snuggled up with blankets to rest and relax. With full stomachs and comforting quilts, Mary feared she would fall asleep. It had been an exhausting week, but it was not her desire to fall asleep when she was supposed to be spending quality time with Star.

As the movie started, Mary announced, "If anyone gets hungry, there are plenty of leftovers in the kitchen on the island."

There were a couple of groans and Joseph said, "I don't think I will need to eat again until sometime next week!"

The two couples chuckled, and then grew quiet as the movie began. Mary, surprisingly enough, made it successfully through the first movie. But somewhere during the second one, she lost her battle to keep her eyes open and sleep became the victor.

She awoke with a start at the end of the movie and immediately felt guilty for having fallen asleep.

"Oh, Star," she apologized. "I'm so sorry. I didn't mean to fall asleep."

But Star was still as empathetic as she had always been. "It's okay, Mom," she reassured her. "I know you have had a busy week. And Dad and I enjoyed it anyway."

Looking around, Mary realized that Connor was no longer in the room with them.

"Where did Connor go?" she queried.

Star shot a sheepish glance toward the hallway door and said, "I think he went upstairs to read."

With dusk beginning to settle in, Mary decided the house was getting a little gloomy. She snapped on a couple of lamps, and then decided to go turn a light on in the kitchen in case anyone wanted some leftovers. But when she flipped the switch to the kitchen overhead light, she was greeted with a huge surprise.

There stood Connor, behind the island, sampling the leftovers. But that was not so much of a surprise as what he was wearing, or not wearing, as was the case. Noticing that he was naked from the waist up, Mary quickly looked away. Then drawing in a quick breath, she recovered and returned to meet his gaze.

"Tell me you have something covering your lower half," she said, jokingly and half-heartedly.

Connor paused, a slab of turkey in one hand and a cookie in the other, and then looked slowly down at his lower half. Awkwardly looking back up at his enquirer, he shook his head back and forth to indicate a negative answer.

Mary's natural response was to cover her eyes and call for her husband.

"Joseph!" she called loudly, and sounding in need of an immediate response.

Then, realizing he would see exactly what she was viewing if he came, she thought better of the moment, and decided to escape to the living room. She charged in to face her husband and daughter, while Connor took advantage of the opportunity and ran down the hallway to the stairs leading to the upper level. He was not much more than a blur as he passed the door to the living room, but Joseph happened to catch sight of him.

"What the heck was that?" he demanded.

"That was a streaker," Mary replied.

"In my house?" Joseph questioned.

Mary nodded in the affirmative. They stared at each other momentarily, and then both parents turned to face their daughter.

Star looked first at her mother, and then turned her gaze to her father. Not knowing what to say next, she simply covered her face with her hands and dropped down onto the couch.

Joseph looked at his daughter and said, "Do you want to tell us what is going on here, Star?"

Without looking up or uncovering her face, she said, "Not without Connor."

"Very well," Joseph replied. Walking to the foot of the staircase, he called up, "Connor, could you put some clothes on and come down here, please?"

A few minutes later, Connor came walking down the stairs. He was barefoot, but otherwise clothed. He sheepishly made his way into the living room and quietly sat down beside Star.

Joseph sat down in his recliner and Mary perched uncomfortably on the edge of her overstuffed chair. And there they sat, wanting an explanation, but yet not really wanting to know. Finally, Star mustered up the courage to tell them the secret she had dreaded to admit.

"Connor and I live in a nudist camp," she stated, careful

not to make eye contact with either parent.

Joseph groaned and looked away, while Mary only covered her mouth with her hand and gave a small gasp.

"How long has this been going on?" Joseph questioned dryly.

"Ever since we met a few years ago," Star stated.

"Well, you sure had us fooled," Joseph scoffed.

Star looked up with a hurt expression, so Mary stepped in with a softer approach.

"Why, Star?" she gently questioned.

Star looked empathetically at her mother and said, "You know I have never liked wearing clothes, Mom."

Mary thought back to all the times she had had to put Star's clothes back on her when she was younger. But she had thought it was just a stage she was going through. Certainly she would outgrow it.

Star continued, "And remember every time you bought me new clothes, I couldn't wear them....."

"....until I cut the tags out," Mary finished for her daughter. She had never had trouble identifying Star's clothes. They were the ones that were always missing the tags.

"But to live in a nudist camp," Joseph insisted. "With people running around naked? I just can't picture my little girl doing that."

"I'm sorry to disappoint you, Dad," Star said, looking close to tears.

"I don't know that it's disappointing so much as it is a surprise," Mary said, trying to keep her daughter from crying.

There was a long, awkward silence, and then Connor spoke up.

"If you'll excuse me," he politely said, "I think I will go upstairs and read."

Mary and Joseph nodded, and he stood up to leave. Taking his hand, Star stood up as well.

"I think I'll join you," she said. "That way my parents can have a few moments to themselves."

Pausing at the hallway door, Star turned to look at her

parents.

"We can still stay for the night, can't we?" she asked.

"Of course you can, sweetie," her mother replied. "We're not going to kick you out."

"Just keep your clothes on," Joseph added.

After they left the room, Mary and Joseph sat in stunned silence. It was Mary who was first to speak up.

"I can't believe Star lives like that," she said mellowly.

"It's definitely not anything I would have expected either," Joseph agreed.

Mary sat in a state of complete dejection. She felt totally helpless, not having the energy to save this day, or knowing how to do it even if she did. Joseph sat for a moment longer, and then decided he needed a change of scenery.

"I'm going to get a snack," he announced.

As he got up to head for the kitchen, the doorbell rang. He paused for a moment, but Mary waved him on stating she would get it. So he headed out toward the kitchen and she for the front door.

Mary opened the door with anticipation, hoping whoever was on the other side had some good news for her. But she almost let out an audible groan when she saw Margaret Wellington standing there. Of all people to show up at her front door at a time like this! Margaret was probably the last person she wanted to see!

"Oh, Mary," smiled Margaret, in her artificial manner. "So nice to see you. I've brought a fruitcake for you and Joey."

She held out the fruitcake, looking around Mary to see if she could spot Joseph. When Mary failed to take the cake, Margaret returned her gaze to her and briefly studied her face.

"Why, Mary," she said, "You look absolutely terrible. What seems to be the matter?"

Mary gulped and stuttered, but couldn't seem to make anything intelligible come out of her mouth.

Setting the fruitcake on the stand beside the door, Margaret took Mary's arm and said, "Come sit down, Mary, and tell me what is wrong."

She led her to a chair in the living room and pulled another one close so she could comfort her. She rubbed Mary's back and reassured her that it couldn't be that bad.

Mary was surprised at her behavior. She had never seen a compassionate side to Margaret Wellington. Seeing the look of concern on Margaret's face and with the stress of the past eleven days, Mary suddenly broke. She just couldn't take anymore.

Before she knew what she was doing, she was spilling her soul to Margaret Wellington. She sobbed out her heartaches and failures of being a mother of twelve. She told her of the shock of learning that Star lives in a nudist camp. Star's day wasn't going well, and she still had to get through the tree lighting with Joy tomorrow. Margaret sat quietly, handing Mary a tissue and seeming to take everything in.

When Mary finished her spiel, she blew her nose and waited for words of comfort. But in her state of distress, she had forgotten who she was talking to. Not hearing any words of reassurance, she wiped her eyes and glanced up at Margaret.

Margaret had a perplexed look on her face. Seeing Mary looking at her, she straightened her back and looked past Mary as if she wasn't there.

"It must make you feel like a failure having a child who lives in a nudist camp," Margaret plainly stated.

Mary dried her eyes, blew her nose, and shot a sideways glance at Margaret. *Why did I just bare my soul to her like that?* she asked herself. She had just been caught off guard in a moment of weakness, she reasoned with herself.

When Mary failed to respond, Margaret continued with her reprimand. "You should have never had so many children, Mary," she stated frankly. "It was my choice to not have any. Children take up too much of your time and energy. They are noisy and unpredictable, even after they grow up, as you have found out. Thank goodness I had common sense enough to not have any. Kids simply wear you out!"

Rising from her chair, Margaret paused for a moment,

looked directly at Mary with her condescending manner and added, "Which is probably why you look so worn out all the time, because you had so many."

And with that, she turned and marched toward the door. Mary stood and numbly followed her out of the living room. She was already despising herself for having spilled her guts to the likes of Margaret Wellington, and worrying about what repercussions she would face because of it.

When she reached the door, Margaret turned to face Mary.

"I have more fruitcakes to deliver, so I must be on my way," she announced. Then, seeing the look of concern on Mary's face, she said, "You only have one more day to get through, Mary. You'll survive."

Margaret nonchalantly drifted out the front door, and Mary had to fight the urge to slam the door behind her. She watched through the window as Margaret seemed to glide effortlessly and unconcerned to her car parked in the yard. Then Mary let out with an almost inhuman half scream, half howl. The noise brought both Joseph and Star running.

Joseph arrived first and seeing his wife's obvious distress, he naturally questioned, "What happened?"

Mary turned to look at her husband with fire in her eyes. Not just a family-friendly campfire, but a full-fledged four alarm conflagration.

"Margaret Wellington, that's what happened!" Mary yelled, as if the name alone could explain the depth of her frustrations.

"Oh...." Joseph said softly, trying to surmise what the problem was. Mary had not been in a good frame of mind when he left the room. The doorbell must have been an unexpected visit from Margaret, and a "friendly" visit from Margaret Wellington was not exactly what his wife had needed right now.

Joseph turned to look at Star, who stood wide-eyed and silent by the door to the living room. It was almost as if she was afraid to enter the room. It was not often that she

194

saw her mother this upset, and she felt she might have a lot to do with her current dilemma.

Turning back to his wife, Joseph was surprised to see her donning her coat and gloves. He wasn't sure Mary was in any condition to go anywhere right now.

"Where are you going?" he asked cautiously. He wanted to discourage her from leaving the house, but also knew that he had to be tender with her in her present state of mind.

"I have wanted to get over to Miss Lighthart's house all week to bring her a peace treaty for the way our grandchildren treated her on Sunday," she explained, struggling to get her glove on. After a few seconds of trying, Mary gave up and threw her glove across the hallway.

Joseph grimaced, but said nothing. When Mary started throwing things, she was close to rock bottom. During times like these, he had usually come up with a project in his workshop that needed his immediate attention. Giving her space and time to recover had always seemed to work in the past. But this time, she was heading out the door.

"This fruitcake would make an excellent gift for Miss Lighthart, if I do say so myself," Mary continued, seeming very pleased with herself for thinking of it.

"What if Margaret already gave her one?" Joseph asked.

Mary looked at him, as if she hadn't thought of that yet, but then quickly recovered. "Then she will have two," she said with a sarcastic smirk.

Joseph couldn't think of a way to convince her that maybe this could wait until later when she was feeling better. He was concerned that Mary was too upset to be driving. But if there was one thing Joseph had learned in over forty years of marriage was that when Mary determined to do something, there was no changing her mind.

So he simply pursed his lips, nodded and said, "Okay, but are you sure you don't want to wait until you have calmed down a bit?"

Mary looked at Joseph as if he had two heads. "I have got to get this fruitcake out of my house," she insisted, "and the sooner, the better!"

She paused and looked from Joseph to the troubled face of her daughter standing behind him.

"Even if I just take it outside, put it behind the wheel of the car, and back over it!" she stated loudly. "It's got to go somewhere! Haggie, Naggie, Maggie's fruitcake is not staying in my house!!"

And with that, she picked up the fruitcake, stormed out the door, and slammed it vehemently behind her.

If it hadn't been such a dire situation, Joseph would have chuckled. It was like she was taking all her frustrations from the past eleven days out on that poor, innocent fruitcake. One would have thought the fruitcake was made of deadly poison, or a high-level of explosives, the way she was so desperate to get rid of it.

After Mary's dramatic exit, Star looked to her father, wondering what they should do.

"Is she going to be okay?" she asked.

Joseph reached out to his daughter and pulled her close to give her a hug. "You know your mother," he said, reassuringly. "She's a very resilient person. She'll bounce back from this in no time."

"I hope so," Star said, clearly not as convinced as her father.

Joseph just smiled and kissed her forehead, not really sure of it himself. If Mary didn't return shortly, he would organize a search party and go find her.

****

A short time later, Mary returned from her plight to free herself of Margaret Wellington's fruitcake. Joseph was sitting in his recliner, reading the newspaper. Star was on the couch, where she had been trying to wait patiently for her mother's return, but had not been winning the battle. She had felt almost physically ill from worrying. Connor, feeling like he was the root of the current dilemma, had chosen to remain hidden in the bedroom upstairs.

Mary casually removed her coat and hung it in the closet in the hallway, then walked into the living room and perched on the edge of her overstuffed chair. Her face was drawn, and she looked emptied and drained of her usual zest for life.

"How did everything go?" Joseph asked, looking at his exhausted wife over the top of the newspaper.

"Okay," Mary said weakly.

"Had Margaret already given her a fruitcake?" Star asked quietly, not sure if she should participate in the conversation or just stay small and out of sight.

Mary turned to look at Star, almost as if she hadn't realized she was there. She knew it wasn't fair to take her frustrations out on those she loved most. It wasn't Star's fault that the last week and a half had been so demanding. Nor was it her fault that Mary was the mother of twelve children, who now had spouses and grandchildren that were challenging to keep up with. It was true that having so many children had been her choice. Even though it made for a hectic lifestyle, and had proven to be a painful process lately, she knew deep inside that she wouldn't have traded it for the world.

So Mary relaxed a bit and smiled at Star. "No, not yet," she replied. "If she plans on bringing one to her, then I must have gotten there first."

"Well, there," said Star, trying to cheer her mother up. "You finally beat Haggie, Naggie, Maggie at something!"

Everyone chuckled, and then Mary grew quiet once more. There was an awkward silence before Mary spoke up again.

"You know, on the way home, I was thinking that I'm a lot like a turtle," she said, kind of dreamily and looking off into space.

Creasing his forehead, Joseph gave his wife a

questioning glance and set his newspaper down to wait for an explanation. Star looked from mother to father, not quite sure where this conversation was going, and wondering if her mother might be having some kind of a break down.

Mary seemed temporarily lost in her thoughts. Neither Joseph or Star dared to interrupt her, though. They just waited patiently, interested in learning exactly how Mary thought she resembled a turtle.

Finally Joseph prodded her, "And what makes you think you're like a turtle?"

Mary looked at him blankly, almost as if she had forgotten the point of her conversation.

"Well, for one thing, they don't move very fast," she replied. "Sometimes I feel like I'm at a slow crawl, too."

Joseph didn't really see the connection. His wife was always on the run and even at her age, she could be challenging to keep up with. Why did she feel her life was at a slow crawl? But he felt it was best to not question her just yet.

Mary stared at the ceiling as she spoke, either not wanting to face her audience, or maybe speaking more to herself. Both parties quietly and patiently listened to her analogy.

"The only way for a turtle to move forward is for him to come out of his shell, right?" she questioned, looking first at her husband and then toward her daughter.

Her gaze lingered on Star, who timidly replied, "Uh-huh."

Seemingly satisfied with the answer, Mary continued. "Well, it seems to me that every time I come out of my shell in an effort to move forward, someone whacks me over the head again!"

She suddenly seemed to spring back to life. She jumped to her feet, marched toward the hallway door and paused long enough to finish her tirade.

"So I am going to tuck my aching head back into the safety of my shell and go soak in the bathtub!" And with that, she ascended the stairs methodically and disappeared into the darkness.

Star's eyes were open wide with concern. She looked at her father and said, "Are you going to go talk to her?"

Joseph looked toward the staircase, where he had last seen his wife, then turned back toward his daughter.

"I'll go check on her in a minute," he told her. "But I think right now, she needs some time to herself."

"So what did she mean?" Star asked her dad. "Did she mean that I whacked her over the head?"

Joseph looked tenderly at his concerned daughter. Learning that she lived in a nudist camp had been a real shock to both parents, but he didn't want Star to feel bad. He knew the trials and problems Mary had faced in recent days, and Star's news had just been one more blow for her to deal with. And since he never wanted his children to feel like they were at fault for the challenges he and Mary faced as parents, he would use his typical escape.

"I don't think she meant you, honey," he reassured her. "I think she was referring to her interactions with Margaret Wellington. You know how Margaret has always been a thorn in your mother's side, and right now she feels bad for having shared personal information with her."

"Did she tell Margaret that I live in a nudist camp?" Star asked, alarmed.

Joseph didn't want to admit that she could have, nor was he really certain, so he only said, "It's possible."

"Oh, no," Star said with dismay, "now the whole town will know."

She paused to think of the repercussions of Margaret Wellington knowing her personal secret. The more she thought of it, the more upset she became. Finally, she blurted out her frustration.

"Why can't that woman mind her own business?" she stated. "I hate her!"

Joseph looked at Star in surprise. He couldn't remember her every saying anything like that before. But on the other hand, he knew it was a vented comment. Margaret had trespassed on their family business, and her visit had triggered a negative ending to what was supposed to be a special day for Star. He would admit that he didn't care for Margaret Wellington, either, but Star's comment needed attention. And in an effort to always be a guiding light for his children, he knew he had to correct Star's thought process.

"We don't hate Margaret Wellington," he said gently to his daughter. Then picking up his newspaper and trying to find where he had left off, he ended with, "We just strongly dislike her!"

****

While Mary bathed, Star popped another movie into the DVD player. She tried to relax, but found it hard to focus on the storyline. Her concern for the current situation outweighed the antics of one of her favorite childhood movies.

Relief flooded over her when she heard her mother coming down the stairs and saw her enter the room. Mary looked refreshed, almost like a new person.

"How are you feeling, Mom?" she asked softly.

"Much better, sweetie," Mary said, coming over to kiss her daughter on the top of her head.

Joseph looked her way and said, "You look more relaxed. That bath must have done you a world of good."

"It did indeed," Mary agreed. Turning to face Star, she said, "I just remembered I was supposed to make some goodies for the tree lighting tomorrow. Are you up to doing some baking?"

"You bet I am," Star smiled, feeling so much better just seeing her mother back in her normal state of mind.

The remainder of the evening was filled with a myriad of laughter and fun, flour and sugar. They baked brownies and chocolate chip cookies, and whipped up a couple of batches of cupcakes. As the night grew longer, the two women became tired and silly. While frosting and decorating a batch of cookies, they reached the level of being just plain foolish.

Picking up a gingerbread man, Star said, "Let's pretend this one is Margaret Wellington."

She proceeded to break a leg off and said, "Take that Naggie Maggie!"

Both mother and daughter burst into laughter. Hearing their merriment from the living room, Joseph decided to check in on them and remind them of how late the hour was. He stepped into the kitchen just in time to see his wife's comeback.

"No, this is even better," Mary said. She bit the head off and with a muffled cry, said, "Oh, Joey, save me!"

The women burst into another round of laughter. They turned to Joseph to see his reaction. He only shook his head and said, "You two are hopeless!"

When Joseph saw the flour and cooking utensils on the counter, it reminded him of Luke's day when Mary had thrown a cup of flour at him. He decided to exit before she remembered it, too. In her goofy state of mind, she might just try it again.

He turned to walk away and said, "I'm going to bed before you bite my leg off, too!"

He headed down the hallway leading to the upper level. As he did, he heard the two women whispering. Then a noise behind him caught his attention. He turned around just in time to see a measuring cup bouncing off the wall and rolling across the floor. He momentarily contemplated returning to the kitchen to ask what that was all about, but then he heard two peals of hilarious laughter coming from the kitchen.

He wondered if they had both gone insane, but at least they were having a good time. He decided it was probably best if he just let them be.

Rather than questioning it, he simply called out, "Good night, ladies!"

Star, feeling the need to explain her actions, called back, "Sorry, Dad. It just slipped out of my hand."

And then they were roaring in laughter again.

"Right, Star, I'm sure it did," Joseph called back to her, as he headed down the hallway.

Then starting up the stairs, Joseph shook his head and muttered to himself, "Like mother, like daughter!"

******

****

Joy

****

Chapter 13
Joy

✯✯✯✯✯✯✯

It was finally Day Twelve, the day Mary had been waiting for. She awoke to a whirlwind of emotions. For one thing, she was relieved that this was the last day before her life would return to normalcy. Plus, she was excited that this was the day of the community tree lighting. She had high hopes for a fun-filled evening with Joy and her children.

Yet, on the other hand, she dreaded seeing Margaret Wellington. Not only would she be portraying Mrs. Claus and pretending to be married to Joseph, but she now knew family secrets that were none of her business. That could be dangerous information in her hands, and Mary's family could easily be exploited.

And then there was Star, Mary thought to herself. They had enjoyed their baking time together last night, but the thought of her little girl returning to a community where clothing was obsolete was hard for her to think about.

Joseph rolled over to face his wife.

"Are you awake?" he asked sleepily.

"Yes," Mary replied. "Just thinking about the hopes for today and remembering the disaster of yesterday."

"Yesterday was a challenge," Joseph agreed.

"Thinking about my baby living in a nudist camp almost makes me want to stay in bed today," Mary sighed. Brightening up, she asked, "Do you think we could call in sick?!"

Joseph smiled at his wife's humor. "We still have houseguests sleeping down the hall," he reminded his wife.

"That's true," Mary remembered, and then added, "Plus, Joy needs our help today." She turned to face her husband and asked, "How was Star after I bailed out on you guys last night?"

"She was okay," Joseph said, reflectively. "We let Margaret Wellington take the blame for most of yesterday's disaster, so she expressed some bad feelings toward her."

"Margaret Wellington," Mary said, letting out a long, slow sigh. "How will I ever face her again?"

"Simple," Joseph said, leaning over to kiss his wife's forehead. "Just ignore her."

Mary looked at her husband like he had just come out of a padded cell. "And how, exactly, do I do that?" she demanded. "She is playing Mrs. Claus tonight, pretending she is married to my husband!"

Joseph only chuckled. "Well, it's obvious that I can't avoid her. But you can stay with Joy and the kids and away from 'Mrs. Claus.'"

"You bet I'll avoid her," said Mary, climbing out of bed and bending over to retrieve her slippers. Standing back up to face her husband, she added, "Like she's got the Coronavirus."

Joseph only chuckled again. He had always loved his wife's sense of humor, but he could top that one.

"And as soon as the tree lighting is over, I will be sure to file for a divorce from Mrs. Claus," he informed her.

Picking up a pillow, Mary playfully whopped her husband over the head with it.

"You bet you will," she said, throwing on a robe and heading off to make breakfast for her houseguests.

****

Mary made a hearty breakfast for the guests still sleeping in their rooms upstairs. Maybe Star's visit had not reached the level Mary had hoped for, but at least she had been fed well.

Star and Connor appeared in the kitchen a short time later. The aroma of pancakes, bacon, sausage and fresh-brewed coffee had stirred them from their slumber and drawn them to the kitchen.

Mary greeted her daughter with a smile, and promptly

announced they would not be eating gingerbread men for breakfast. Connor looked quizzically at Star, who only giggled and said she would explain it to him later.

Soon the group was dining around the table, laughing and conversing as jovial as the day before. Mary and Joseph shared how this was Joy's day, and they would be helping her with the annual tree lighting on the common.

"Dad is going to be Santa," Mary informed them.

Star smiled at her father and said, "I wish we could stay to see it." Looking at Connor, she added, "But we must be on our way."

He returned her smile and nodded in agreement.

"Guess who is playing Mrs. Claus," Mary said, looking at her houseguests to see who would wager a guess.

Star had just taken a big bite of pancake and had been plainly taught that it is not polite to speak with a full mouth. She naturally assumed it would be her mother, so she simply pointed a finger at her.

Joseph chuckled and said, "Good guess, but it's not your mother."

Star turned questioningly to her mother, who rolled her eyes and groaned, "Margaret Wellington!"

"No way!" said Star, clearly surprised by the response.

Star had shared her thoughts and frustrations over the behavior of Margaret Wellington with Connor last night, so he had formed his own conclusions regarding her nature and personality.

Looking down at his plateful of food, Connor said, "That should be illegal."

When no one responded, he looked up to find all eyes focused on him. Quick to defend himself, he added, "I mean, Mrs. Claus is supposed to be friendly and kind, right? Just like Santa. That doesn't really sound like Margaret Wellington to me!"

Mary, Joseph, and Star burst into laughter. It hadn't taken long for Connor to figure Margaret out.

After their time around the breakfast table, Star and

Connor gathered their belongings (what few they had) and said their good-byes. Star wished "Santa" and Mary good luck with the tree lighting, encouraging her mother to keep her distance from "Mrs. Claus." She encouraged her father to try to at least be civil to his "wife" for the evening.

When they had departed, Mary returned to the kitchen to clean up. Joseph came in later to find her smiling as she washed a sink full of dirty dishes.

"I didn't know you liked washing dishes so much," he joked with her.

"I'm just feeling better, knowing that Star left on a good note," she replied. "Last night was a bit of a disaster, with my overreacting to Star's news and the unexpected visit from Margaret. We had a good time baking, though."

Turning to face her husband, she added, "Which is good, because I never want to send my children away unhappy."

She continued to smile as she cleared scraps of uneaten food into the trash can. Looking up at Joseph, she added, "And today is our last day. Tomorrow, our lives will be back to normal. We have conquered this twelve day adventure!"

Joseph smiled at her optimism. He didn't want to discourage her, but they weren't done yet. And anything could happen, as they had already learned.

Giving his wife a quick hug, he said, "The day is still young, my darling. We still have the adventures of tonight to get through."

****

They had agreed to meet Joy on the town common at noon to help set up. Joy and her husband, Seth, had already managed to put the lights on the tree, but there were still areas where help was needed. The gazebo needed to be decorated and a visitor's station set up where the children could sit and visit with Santa.

Joy had been excited with her purchase of a dozen giant candy canes. Those needed to be set up along the walkway leading up to the Christmas tree. Plus, they would need to organize the snack area, where people could get hot chocolate and baked goods to munch on.

The plan was to have Santa and Mrs. Claus arrive in a horse-drawn wagon. With the townspeople assisting in the countdown, Santa would magically light the tree. Of course, Seth would secretly be assisting Santa with this task by manning the electrical outlet. Once the tree was lit, everyone would join together in singing a few Christmas carols around the tree. Then they would be on their own, taking turns with the horse-drawn wagon rides, visiting with Santa to get bags of candy and have their picture taken with him, or enjoying some hot drinks and refreshments.

It all sounded like so much fun to Mary. And there had been a lot of planning that went into it. How could anything possibly go wrong? she wondered to herself.

Joy smiled and waved to her parents from her position in the gazebo, centrally located on the common. She and Seth were surrounded by piles of Christmas decorations – red and silver garland, strings of Christmas lights needing to be hung, red velvet bows and glittering snowflakes. It was her goal to transform the plain, ordinary town gazebo and common into a magical winter wonderland for the children. And it appeared that she had enough decorations to do it.

"Looks like we have our work cut out for us," Mary said to Joseph, smiling and returning her daughter's cheerful wave. "But we can do it, right Mrs. Davis?" Joseph returned. "Remember, it's for the kids….and this is day number twelve."

"Hallelujah!" Mary joked.

But decorating did not prove to be as challenging as Mary and Joseph had expected. The adults laughed and joked while they hung lights and strung garland. Joy's in-laws had agreed to watch her children, Caleb and Jordan, to allow the adults to focus on some serious decorating time. When they had finished, the couples stood back and admired their work.

"Well, I think you did it, Joy," Mary commented, proud of her daughter's creativity. "This does look magical. The kids are going to love it."

Mary turned to face her daughter, pride of her creativity and involvement in the community plainly written on her face. She gave her a hug and said, "You are amazing!"

She turned to the two men, arched her shoulders with excitement, and said, "This is going to be so much fun. I can hardly wait. I almost feel like a kid again!"

"Speaking of kids," Joy spoke up, "We should probably go get ours."

With the decorating completed and time drawing close for the beginning of the ceremony, the two couples decided to take a break for a quick bite to eat. Since the costumes were at Joy's house, they would dine there.

Seth and Joseph volunteered to pick the kids up. Joy and Mary would stop and grab some take-out food. Then they would meet back at the house, have a quick meal, and prepare for the final touches for the evening.

****

Mary and Joy arrived back at the house first. They started setting the table and preparing for a quick meal of fast food. They had just finished setting up the food when the rest of the gang arrived.

Jordan and Caleb rushed into the room to give Grandma Mary a hug.

"Grandma!" they shouted, attacking her with hugs from either side.

They all settled at the table and chatted happily during their meal. As they were finishing, Joy turned her attention to the children.

"I need your help with a little secret tonight," she informed them. "You know how Santa is very busy at this time of the year, right?"

The children nodded their heads, anxious for their mother to continue. They loved secrets, and very were excited that they would be participating in one.

"So you know that Santa is supposed to be at the tree lighting ceremony," Joy continued. "The real Santa was too busy to come, so I found someone else to help us out. Do you have any guesses who it might be?"

Caleb looked innocently at his mother and asked, "You?"

Everyone around the table chuckled. Then Joy turned to her son and asked, "Do I really look like Santa?"

Caleb shook his head and his cheeks flushed a bit. Mary was quick to come to the rescue of her red-faced grandson.

"You were close, though," she reassured him. "It is someone in this room."

The children looked around the room and, knowing it was just their parents and grandparents at the table, they looked expectantly from face-to-face. Grandpa Joseph's face beamed, and was a dead give away.

In unison, the two children piped out, "Grandpa Joseph?!"

Grandpa Joseph smiled at his grandchildren and said, "You guessed it!"

Seth looked at his two young children and said, "But, remember - it's a secret. No one can know about it."

"That's right," Joy added. "You can't tell anyone that Santa is really Grandpa Joseph tonight."

"Do you think you can keep our little secret?" Grandma Mary asked her grandchildren.

Caleb and Jordan looked at each other with glee in their eyes. Then turning back to the adults, they motioned as if zipping their lips, signaling their vow of silence. Everyone laughed freely and Joy pushed away from the table.

"Okay, then it's time to get ready to go," she announced. "I have to put my elf suit on. I am going to be Santa's helper."

"Does anyone want to watch Santa put his suit on?" Grandpa Joseph asked.

"Yes!" the two kids chorused together.

"Then come with me," he said, standing up and exiting the room.

Caleb and Jordan quickly jumped up to follow him. Mary decided to join them as well, in case "Santa" needed any help.

"I'll come, too," she said, hurrying to catch up with them.

Jordan turned to her grandmother and asked, "So, does this mean you are going to be Mrs. Claus?"

Grandma Mary almost groaned, thinking about the woman who would be playing Mrs. Claus tonight. But she was too excited about the events that lay ahead of them to let it put a damper on the happy atmosphere.

"No, not tonight," she said.

Caleb looked at his grandparents and asked, "Then who is going to be Mrs. Claus?"

Joy explained that Margaret Wellington from the church had volunteered to play the part.

Processing it for a moment, Jordan looked up and said, "So, Grandpa's going to be married to someone else tonight?"

The adults all looked briefly at each other, and then Joy said, "Sort of."

Grandma Mary smiled at her grandchildren's confused faces, and in an attempt to explain, she said, "It's kind of like being in a play. They are just playing a part. It's not really real."

"Good," Caleb said, looking up at his grandparents, "'cause I wouldn't want Mrs. Wellington for a grandmother!"

"Let's be nice, Caleb," Joy reprimanded her son. She placed her hands on his shoulders to point him in the right direction and edged him along toward the Christmas costumes awaiting them. As she wandered past her mother, she whispered, "Smart boy!"

Grandma Mary smiled and the group headed to don their costumes in preparation of the festivities ahead of them.

A short time later, Grandpa Joseph reappeared as Santa and Joy was dressed as his helper – complete with a green and red outfit, pointed hat and even elf boots with a curly, pointed toe.

After taking pictures of Santa, his elf and the grandchildren, the group hopped into their cars and headed into the center of town. They dropped "Santa" off at the horse barn, where he would meet up with "Mrs. Claus" and would then continue to the common by horse-drawn wagon.

****

Once at the common, Mary and Joy began setting up the snacks. Caleb and Jordan were so excited, they could hardly contain themselves. When some of their friends started to arrive, they wanted to go play with them while waiting for the festivities to begin.

"Can we go play while we wait for Grandpa Joseph to come?" Caleb asked.

Both Grandma Mary and Joy were quick to remind them of their secret. Holding up a finger in front of her lips, Joy said, "Shh! Remember our secret."

The children both threw a hand over their mouths, surprised that they had already forgotten. They looked at each other, smiled, then again motioned that their lips were zipped. With that, they ran off to join their friends, who were enjoying the new magical appearance of the common.

Soon the common was bustling with children, families, and area residents who had come to participate in the holiday event. The air was alive with excitement and anticipation, with everyone anxiously awaiting the arrival of Santa and the magical moment when he would light the tree. Children's gleeful voices rang out in laughter and camaraderie, accompanied by parents greeting friends and sharing holiday cheer.

Sharply at 6:30, the sound of sleigh bells could be heard in the distance, along with the clomping of horse hoof beats. Not wanting the children to miss Santa's arrival, Joy decided to call their attention to the approaching wagon.

"Look everyone," she called out, pointing to the horse-drawn wagon coming their way. "It looks like Santa and Mrs. Claus are coming!"

The crowd turned their attention to the approaching wagon, and a wave of excitement could be heard passing through the children in the crowd. Like a magnet, the crowd drew closer to the approaching wagon, and then parted to make a path for Santa and Mrs. Claus to walk through. The jovial couple in red greeted the children, and gradually made their way to the unlit tree, which waited to join the festival of lights that were already decorating the common.

After allowing time for the children to welcome Santa and Mrs. Claus, Santa's elf called the participants over to the tree to start the countdown.

"Come on over and gather around the tree," Joy called out. "Santa is going to help us light it, and then we will all join in singing some Christmas Carols."

Santa and Mrs. Claus moved over to join Joy beside the tree. Then Joy gave further instructions to the awaiting crowd.

"Let's start at five and count down," she told them. "Then Santa will wave his hand and magically light our tree."

Some of the children looked at each other, wondering how Santa could do that. Seeing their apprehension, Joy looked at them and asked, "Do you think Santa can do that?"

One little girl in the crowd piped up and said, "Sure he can. He's Santa, and Santa is magical!"

"He sure is," said Joy, turning to her father and giving him a smile.

"Okay, here we go," Joy said, holding up her hand to show all five fingers.

Suddenly she thought of Seth, wondering if he was at his post and ready to plug the tree in. A wave of panic swept over her when she saw him chatting with friends, apparently not even aware that the countdown was about to begin.

Looking his way, Joy loudly called out, "Okay, we are going to start the count down!"

Fortunately, she was able to catch his attention. However, he would need to sprint to make it to the outlet in time. Joy knew she needed to stall as long as possible.

"Okay, is everyone ready?" she asked.

The children nodded eagerly, some calling out verbally with affirmation.

"Okay, here we go," she said, looking past the crowd to check on the status of her husband's location.

"Five…four….," she began, panic again welling up when she realized her husband had not reached his goal yet.

"Three………two………..," she slowed the count, trying to stall for time.

Seeing that Seth had reached the outlet, she took a chance that he had found the extension cord and ended with, "one…."

Joy closed her eyes, not wanting to see the disappointment on the children's faces if the tree failed to light. However, a chorus of cheers and whistles circulated through the crowd, signaling success. Joy opened her eyes and smiled with contentment when she observed the lighted tree beside her. She turned to look at her husband, who was winded from his sprint, and gave him a wave of appreciation.

The crowd then joined in a few rounds of festive, lively Christmas Carols, ending on a more mellow note with Silent Night. After the singing ended, Joy dismissed them to enjoy the refreshments, take turns on the horse-drawn wagon ride, and pose for pictures with Santa and Mrs. Claus.

After seating Santa and Mrs. Claus on benches by the newly lit tree, Joy stayed close to make sure there were enough candy bags for the children and to help organize the line. Mary went to watch over the refreshment tables and serve hot chocolate for the chilled participants. Seth went to manage the line at the wagon ride and help the riders get on and off.

During a pause at the refreshment tables, Mary looked

around and marveled. So many emotions floated through her, it was hard to sort them all out. She was so proud of her daughter – for her organizational skills, and for making this happen. She was excited for the children, thinking of the fun they were having and the fond childhood memories they were creating.

A brief moment of negativity passed through her as she looked at Mrs. Claus, knowing it was Margaret Wellington. For one thing, she didn't deserve the honor of playing Mrs. Claus. But more than that, she was pretending to be married to her husband.

It was an emotion that Mary quickly dismissed. She knew it would only last for another hour or two, and then Joseph would be hers again. It wasn't worth letting the thought upset the fun-filled activities of the evening.

Finally, Mary thought how wonderful that they had truly saved the best day for last. The past eleven days had definitely been more of a challenge than she had anticipated, but the twelfth day was going awesome. It had been nothing but fun from the start, and it meant that their twelve day ordeal would end on a positive note.

****

Who knows if fate read Mary Davis's thoughts and determined to burst her bubble of happiness, or if it was just the course of nature. But in a moment of time, it all came crashing down around her.

Everything was going fine until Buzzy arrived. It was hard to believe that with so much joy, festivity and happiness floating through the crowd of participants, that all it took was one twenty pound bulldog to end it all.

At first, Buzzy just circulated through the crowd. Children and residents bent down to pet and greet him. Having been in the area for years, he was well known by most of the residents, so they just let him wander. He wagged his tail and sniffed resident after resident, seeming like nothing more than a harmless and friendly, little dog. But that all changed when he reached the Christmas tree.

As soon as he spotted Joy in her elf suit, standing beside Santa and Mrs. Claus, his whole demeanor changed. His body stiffened, he bared his teeth and then uttered a low, vicious sounding growl. Buzzy was instantly in full attack mode.

Joy was his first victim. She was the closest target, and he seemed to especially dislike her shoes with the curly, pointed toes. He started barking ferociously, nipping at her ankles and biting her shoes. Santa was quick to come to his daughter's rescue.

"Stop it, Buzzy," he commanded, hoping Buzzy would recognize his voice. But Buzzy only saw the costumes, and Joseph's words fell on deaf ears.

Mrs. Claus, being Margaret Wellington and feeling she could control any situation, joined in the battle.

"Buzzy, what is wrong with you?" she asked. She bent over, as if to pick him up, but Joseph cautioned her not to.

"He hates uniforms and costumes," he quickly warned her. "He's not rational when he's in a mood like this."

Knowing that he had to do something quickly to rescue his daughter from this animal who had become deranged and insane, Joseph did the first thing that came to mind. He grabbed one of Joy's giant candy canes and poked Buzzy with it. But just poking didn't deter his actions. So he hit him a little harder.

Buzzy paused when he felt the strike, and then turned his attention to Santa. He didn't like his costume any better than Joy's elf outfit.

Buzzy unleashed his full fury on Joseph, biting at his ankles. His attack grew more vicious by the second. Like a crazy, rabid animal, he began to throw his whole body weight at Santa.

Joseph had had enough of this behavior. He had never seen Buzzy act this poorly before. He had become dangerous and needed to be stopped before he hurt someone. So

Joseph whacked him a little harder with the candy cane. The blow was harder than Joseph had intended, and it knocked little Buzzy unconscious. His limp body fell into a heap on the cold, frozen ground.

Joseph, Margaret, and Joy stood silently staring at Buzzy, stunned by the events of the past few moments. They weren't sure if they were dreaming, or if it had all really happened.

Margaret spoke up first. "Joey, what have you done to Buzzy?" she questioned.

But it was a question that would go unanswered. In the confusion of the attack, the costumed trio didn't realize that the whole event had been witnessed by a wagon full of children just returning from their ride.

The horse-drawn wagon had reached the common just as Buzzy had begun his attack. The occupants had all watched in stunned silence as Buzzy had first attacked the elf and then Santa himself.

Horror was written on every little face when Santa had struck Buzzy with the candy cane. Buzzy was their neighborhood friend. Santa brought them presents, but he only came once a year. Their loyalty lay with the unconscious dog on the ground, who had apparently been injured by the fat man in the red suit.

After a brief moment of stunned silence, one little boy spoke up.

"Santa killed Buzzy," he stated dryly, still not quite sure that what he had just witnessed was real.
Looking at one another, the kids came up with a unanimous, unspoken plan.

"Let's get him!" one boy shouted, and all the kids jumped to their feet and quickly barreled out of the wagon.

"No!!" Caleb yelled after them. "That's my grandpa. Don't hurt him!!"

But his cry fell on deaf ears. The wagon had emptied in record time, and the children all ran over to pile on top of Santa. Poor Joseph had his back turned toward the wagon, and was completely unaware of the onslaught of attackers heading his way. Before he knew what had hit him, he was on the cold ground under the weight of many kicking, clawing, frenzied children.

Joy, Mary, and Seth quickly ran to rescue poor Joseph. Parents of children in the pile came to help as well, pulling kicking, screaming children off the pile and trying to calm them down.

Margaret Wellington, who wasn't fond of children to begin with, backed away from the chaos before her. She decided to focus her attention on the unconscious dog, to see if there was anything she could do to help him.

She gently shook Buzzy, lifting his legs and trying to see if there was still life within him. A few moments later, she was relieved to see his eyes open. But if she thought he would appreciate her efforts to revive him, she was greatly mistaken. He took one look at her costume, and picked up right where he left off. It started with a growl, then barking, and he was soon attached to the hem of her red furry dress.

Margaret ran off across the common, screaming and trying to free herself of the dog attached to her. Sam, the mailman, saw her dilemma. Having years of experience with Buzzy and his unpredictable behavior, he ran after Margaret to see if he could help.

Mary looked around at the chaos before her. Children were being hauled off by distraught parents, still kicking and screaming. Her husband lay on the ground, not yet free from all the attacking children. The only comical piece to it all was Margaret Wellington running frantically around the common with a crazy, deranged dog attached to her dress and Sam chasing her in an effort to help.

How could this wonderful night have gone so foul? She wondered.

But right now her concern was with her husband, so she ran to see if she could help him. She worried that the attack of the children had injured his back again. Hopefully, they could get him off the ground, and find he would still be able to move.

By the time she arrived at his side, he had been freed of the last attacking child.

"Joseph, are you okay?" she anxiously questioned him. "Can you get up?"

Joseph slowly sat up and did a check of his body parts. Moving his arms and legs, he replied, "I think so."

Seth and Mary helped the wounded Santa struggle to his feet. They brought him to the bench to sit and rest.

"Is your back okay?" Mary questioned, still not sure her husband had faired well.

"I think I'm okay," he reassured her. "Just let me sit here for a moment and rest."

Mary dropped down into her husband's lap, and the struggles of the past twelve days seemed to topple down onto her tired shoulders. Sitting on Santa's lap, she began to wail out her sorrows. Santa wrapped his arms around her and attempted to reassure his distraught wife that everything was okay.

"Why couldn't we have had one day with a happy ending?" she sobbed on Santa's shoulder, taking a break from her sobs long enough to blow her nose. "All I wanted was a special day for each one of my children. A day that would stick in their memory and they would never forget!"

Santa nodded his head in agreement, and said "I think we did that, Mary. I think we definitely gave each of them a day that is going to stay with them for a long time!"

****

Had it not followed such a traumatic event and been the culmination of twelve long, hard days, it would actually have been a comical sight. There sat Mary, a grown woman, with her head on Santa's shoulder sobbing her heart out and telling him all her sorrows.

And if it is true that the things which upset us the most make the funniest memories, as she had told Gloria and Angel just a few days ago, then the Davis family would have twelve days of humorous memories to reminisce and laugh about someday in the future!

****

220

****

The Recovery

****

Chapter 14
The Recovery

☆ ☆ ☆ ☆ ☆ ☆ ☆

If they were still counting days, Day Thirteen had finally arrived, and Mary awoke with a sigh of relief. It was finally over. Her twelve day plan had definitely not progressed according to her liking, but they had somehow managed to survive in spite of it all. They were both still alive, in one piece, and they wouldn't need to worry about Christmas for another year.

Hearing Joseph stir, she turned to face her husband.

"Are you awake?" she asked.

"I guess so," he grunted in return.

"We survived," she sighed out loud. "Somehow, we made it through all twelve days."

"We did," Joseph agreed with his wife, and then added, "Now you can start planning for next year!"

"No way," Mary argued. "I'm not even going to think about it for a long time. I need a vacation."

"Now that sounds like a plan," Joseph smiled. "Where should we go?"

Before Mary could answer, the telephone rang. She looked at her husband in alarm, wondering who would be calling them this early in the morning. Picking up the receiver, she was surprised at the voice on the other end.

"Why, Aunt Helen! How are you?" she asked.

Looking at Joseph, she motioned to the receiver and whispered, "It's your Aunt Helen."

Joseph groaned and covered his head with his pillow. He loved his aunt, but she talked too much, and it was nearly impossible to get her to leave when she stopped by for a visit.

"Oh, you were wanting to stop by to visit today?" he heard his wife saying.

"No!!" Joseph whispered fiercely, jumping out of bed.

Putting his pants on, he looked at his wife and said, "Tell her we won't be home."

Mary nodded in acknowledgement and said, "Well, that would be nice, Aunt Helen, but we won't be home today. We were actually just heading out on a vacation."

There was a pause and Mary, repeating Aunt Helen's question, said "Where are we going?"

She looked at Joseph with a fleeting glance of panic crossing her face. Then she plunged ahead and said, "Bermuda!"

Joseph, anxious to be off on a vacation himself, had said, "Florida!" at the same time.

Mary looked up quickly and added, "Or Florida. We haven't finalized the plans yet, but I need to go so we can finish packing. It was nice talking to you, Aunt Helen, and we will be sure to call you when we get back."

Mary and Joseph flew into action, furiously packing so they could head out on a vacation and get out of town before anyone else called or stopped by to visit.

****

After some hasty phone calls and last minute arrangements, Mary and Joseph finally found themselves seated comfortably on an airplane. As they settled into their flight, Mary pulled out a notepad and began to write.

"So, which are you doing? Are you making plans for next year, or are you writing about the adventures of this Christmas?" Joseph asked.

"Neither," Mary replied. "This is something a little more practical."

Looking over her shoulder, Joseph chuckled when he realized Mary was writing some To-Do lists. There was one list for each of them:

<u>Joseph's To-Do List</u>

Finish taking lights off house
Fix scratch in countertop
Fix cuckoo clock
Reorganize books in library
Fix Vienna vase
Rebuild recycling center
Fix Tiffany lamp

<u>Mary's To-Do List</u>

Buy new inflatable snowman
Dispose of dead bird
Replace fire extinguisher
Rearrange spice rack
Fix lights on Christmas tree
Send Gloria a Thank You note for the tongs
Write notes to each of the children

Joseph paused when he got to the "dead bird" item.

"You haven't gotten rid of Joey's dead bird yet?" he asked.

"What are you supposed to do with a dead bird?" Mary asked.

Joseph shrugged and suggested, "Throw it out in the bushes and let nature take its course, I guess."

Mary wasn't happy with that answer. "I couldn't do that to Joey's bird. I'll figure something out."

"So, whatever happened with the replacement bird?" Joseph asked his wife. "You and Gloria came home laughing about your trip to the mall and putting Margaret in her place, but I never did see a new bird."

"There just wasn't another bird there that looked enough like Banjo that Joey wouldn't notice the difference," Mary explained. "So, we decided we would just keep checking periodically, and hopefully we will find one at some point."

She paused, and then added, "We have time, since Joey won't be home for awhile."

"It's probably a good idea anyway," suggested Joseph. Looking at his wife, he continued, "Just think how many birds you could kill between now and then."

Mary playfully hit her husband across the shoulder and said, "Oh, Joseph!"

"Why, you could actually become a serial bird killer," he continued to joke.

Mary just shook her head, not sure she wanted to play along with him. He was right. She was not good at taking care of animals, and they both knew it. Maybe it was a good thing that they hadn't found a replacement bird.

Returning to the list, Joseph asked, "And why do you need to write to each child?"

Mary shrugged and said, "I need to follow up with them. But I'm not sure if I should thank them for coming, or apologize for all the mishaps."

Joseph and Mary looked at each other for a moment, chuckled, and leaned their heads contently back on the headrests.

Mary sighed and said, "I was telling Olivia the other day that with all I do right, it's just hard to understand why so much goes wrong."

Reaching over to take her hand, Joseph said, "I think that's just life, Mary." He paused and then added, "I think the goal in the game of life is to see how quickly you can get back up after another challenge has knocked you off your feet."

Mary paused to contemplate Joseph's philosophy of life, and then said, "And in my life, I seem to have a lot of challenges."

Joseph smiled and said, "I think we gave birth to twelve of them."

The couple chuckled, and Mary added, "And the collection of 'challenges' seems to be growing all the time."

Mary and Joseph took a moment to reflect on their family brood, and Mary's thoughts took a turn to the pious

Margaret Wellington.

"You know when Margaret stopped by to visit the other day, she told me she intentionally didn't have children because she knew they would be too cumbersome. Maybe I should have been more like her."

Joseph turned to look quizzically at his wife. "Did I just hear you say you wanted to be more like Margaret Wellington? That's a first!"

After a moment, he added, "But do you think it would be comforting to go home to an empty house night after night, with no one waiting to greet you or missing you if you were late?"

Mary sighed, and agreed, "No, that isn't the life for me. I need people in my life to give it meaning."

"And 'people' is just another name for 'challenge,' you know," Joseph smiled at his wit.

Mary knew her husband was right. With so many people in the family, there were bound to be challenges. The more people in the mix, the more confusion and chaos there were destined to be.

Mary said nothing for a moment, then sat up and said, "So here's a plan. Why doesn't Margaret take Buzzy in? That would give him a place to call home, and it would give her someone to come home, too! She seemed to be quite attached to him last night."

"Literally!" Joseph smiled, remembering Buzzy hanging off the hem of Margaret's costume. Then he added, "The last time I saw her, Buzzy was chasing her across the common and Sam, the mailman, was trying to come to her rescue."

Mary smiled and said, "Maybe Sam and Margaret would make a good couple."

Joseph chuckled and said, "Do you think Sam could handle a 'good Christian woman' like that?"

Now it was Mary's turn to look quizzically at her husband.

"Are we talking about the same woman?" she asked. "I meant the busybody who gets involved in every organization in town for the sole purpose of sticking her nose into everybody's business. On second thought, Sam deserves better than that!"

Joseph smiled at his wife's blatant honesty. "Yeah, you're probably right on both counts," he agreed. Then he paused to contemplate Margaret Wellington's qualities. Turning to face his wife, he cautiously added, "You know, Margaret does have some good qualities."

Mary quickly turned to face her husband, like this was a concept she had never considered before.

Quick to defend himself, Joseph added, "She is involved in a lot of organizations that benefit the community. There are many families in the town of Enfield that probably truly appreciate the things she does for them."

Mary said nothing for a moment. Margaret had always been such a thorn in her flesh that she had never really stopped to consider the good she did for the community.

Finally she spoke up. "I guess the piece that matters to me is why she does it. Is she just a nosy person who wants to know everyone's business? Or is she just trying to make herself look better all the time? Or maybe she just wants to keep her foot in the door."

Joseph stopped to think about how many 'doors' Margaret had her foot in, and chuckled out loud.

Looking at Mary, he said, "If she is doing it just to keep her foot in the door, then she must have a lot of feet. Maybe she's a caterpillar!"

Mary laughed at her husband's humor, and paused to picture Margaret with a caterpillar body. Then she brightened and added, "If she is a caterpillar, maybe she will spin herself a cocoon and turn into a beautiful butterfly!"

"Maybe Sam will help her with that," Joseph laughed along with his wife. He paused for a moment, then added, "Heaven knows she could use some help polishing off those rough edges."

Turning to face her husband, Mary said, "Well, you should know. You were married to her!"

Her comment startled Joseph, who had still been picturing Margaret changing from a caterpillar into a beautiful butterfly. But looking at his wife's teasing smile, he quickly caught on to the joke.

"Only for one night, honey," he smiled, settling back into his seat. "Just for one very long night."

Mary decided to put her list away and relax for awhile. Soon she and Joseph were laughing about the events of the past twelve days. They laughed about the flat snowman lying on the front lawn, Joey's love struck bird who wouldn't leave the little cuckoo bird alone, and Spencer emptying the fire extinguisher to save them from the fire on the stovetop.

When it came to Garland's day of sledding, Mary asked, "And what about the 'bump of death'?"

"Ouch!" Joseph said, grabbing his back. "Just thinking about that still hurts!"

The couple had a lot to talk about on their flight. The last twelve days had definitely been full of adventure. As they talked and laughed, they realized they had indeed created a lot of memories. And as Mary had told Gloria, the embarrassing moments in life truly do become things to laugh about in the future.

"Funny how one of the days I dreaded the most actually turned out to be the best one," Mary commented.

Joseph said nothing for awhile, while he contemplated just which day it was that Mary was referring to. When he finally determined he didn't know, he asked, "And which day would that be?"

Mary, apparently lost in her own thoughts, looked blankly at her husband for a moment. Then, picking up the trail of their conversation, she said, "Oh! The day with Nick and Morgan, of course. I was so afraid of having a confrontation with Morgan and her perfectionism. But I think we actually did some bonding."

Joseph smiled fondly at his wife. "You know, I think you did. Maybe she is not as stiff and starchy as you thought."

There was a lull in the conversation as the couple each

reveled in the memories of the past twelve days. Then Mary finally spoke up.

"We really have a wonderful family, don't we, Joseph?" Mary said with a sigh of contentment.

"Indeed we do," Joseph agreed fondly, reaching over to take his wife's hand. "Headed by the most amazing woman of all."

Mary smiled lovingly at her husband, and then they both leaned back against their headrest again. Mary broke the spell of contentment by coming up with the most bizarre comment Joseph had ever heard. "I wish they could come on vacation with us," she said.

Immediately picturing the fiasco of bringing twelve children, their spouses and all the grandchildren on a trip together, Mary's eyes flew open wide. She turned to face her husband, who was already looking at her as if she had lost her mind. After all they had just gone through, he couldn't believe his wife had just said that.

Staring at each other with bare honesty written on their faces, both parents simultaneously said, "Not!!!"

Mary and Joseph giggled like teenagers on their first date, and then decided to settle back and watch the clouds roll by beneath them.

"Where did we decide we were going?" Joseph asked.

"We are going wherever this plane takes us," Mary replied.

"That sounds like a plan to me!" Joseph agreed, as the plane sailed off into the clear blue sky.

****

ACKNOWLEDGEMENTS

✯ ✯ ✯ ✯ ✯ ✯ ✯

I would like to thank my therapist, Leona Brown, for helping me to believe in myself. Without her, this book would probably have never reached completion. She opened my eyes to help me to see that writing is not just good therapy for me. It is my passion and calling in life.

Many thanks to my supportive family: to my sister, Debbe Femiak, for the cover design; to my sister, Linda Wright, for her proofreading skills; and to my niece, Michelle Wright, for her computer skills. Their talents and investments in this book were invaluable and brought it to life. I couldn't have done it without them.

And many thanks to God, who gave me the creative ability to write. He has always been my guide in life, and was instrumental in helping me to connect the dots that led to getting this book published. Many years ago, He told me I had words that needed to be voiced. With His continued guidance, may I have many more words to share, and a lot more stories to tell.

✯ ✯ ✯ ✯ ✯ ✯ ✯

About the Author

Kitty Kaye grew up in a small town in rural New England. Having been raised in a family with six childern, she knew the joys and struggles of being part of a large family.

She has put her heart and soul into giving birth to the Davis family and the challenges they face. They find that what matters most in life is not the outcome, but rather the time and effort we give to show our loved ones how much we care.

✰✰✰✰✰✰✰

About the Illustrator

Debbe Femiak was born with a natural talent for art. She has a degree in Liberal Arts and has studied and taught art in various capacities. She is a multi-media artist and is equally comfortable working with pastels, watercolor, acrylics, and drawing, as well as her long time enjoyment of knitting and crocheting. She currently resides in upstate New York.

✰✰✰✰✰✰✰

OTHER BOOKS BY THE AUTHOR

By Kitty Kaye
Illustrated by Debbe Femiak

Abigail Carter would not deny that she had been blessed with three beautiful children. As a mother, her love for her children was as genuine as it comes. However, it seemed that recently someone had stolen her eldest daughter, Joy, and replaced her with a teenage nightmare. Then when her son, Corey, crashes his ATV into her brand new car and her youngest daughter, Holly, falls out of the tree and breaks her arm, Abigail knows she needs help. Keeping this family safe is beyond her human means.

Her husband, Russell, does all he can to help provide harmony in the family, but it just doesn't seem to be enough. Something has to be done for the safety of her children, and to maintain her sanity. So Abigail goes to the highest power she knows – right to the throne room of God.

At her request, God sends three angels to help out. But will these rusty humans have what it takes to keep them safe? At times, it seems like the heavenly trio has met their match with the three Carter children.

Angels for Abigail *is a fun, fictional story of family trials and the heavenly visitors who are doing their best to try to keep the Carter children on track, safe from themselves, and out of trouble. But which trio will be the victors – the angels, or the kids they were sent to protect?*

Kitty Litter: Thoughts from the Heart *is a sprinkling of uplifting thoughts, designed to give life a fresh, new aroma and help the reader see past the unpleasant aspects of life. It is comprised of three sections:*

- *The Art of Living*
- *The Joys of Parenting*
- *For the Spirit.*

Some thoughts are geared toward encouraging overwhelmed parents. Others are basic thoughts on the components of life itself and things that cross our paths simply as a side effect of being human. Some articles take on a spiritual tone and address the deeper meanings in life.

Wherever you may be on your walk in life, ***Kitty Litter: Thoughts from the Heart*** *has a message for you. Don't give up on this thing called life. It has too much to offer to waste time hanging out in the litter box.*

Let ***Kitty Litter*** *help you muster up some courage, put a smile back on your face, and find the strength to step out of the litter box to give life another chance.*

Cover Illustrated by Debbe Femiak

Jacob Miller was a good kid. He had been born into a respectable family, with loving parents who instilled positive morals and values in him. From the beginning of his life, they had worked hard at teaching him right from wrong. Yet, his childhood hadn't been perfect. Several traumas happened in the early stages of Jacob's childhood that had left him questioning the meaning of life. He had faced sleepless nights and days of heartache as he tried to make sense of it all.

However, Jacob Miller was a resilient child. He had always had a happy-go-lucky attitude, and he knew that he could rise above it all. Life had to have meaning and purpose, and he would figure out where he fit into all of it. As he grew older and became an adult, he determined the hardships of life would not hold him down or lead him astray. He would take charge and find true intention for his life. But, did he control his life, or did life control him?

Thirty Seconds to Life is a story that shows how life can sometimes fall apart, even for those who have had a good upbringing and the best of intentions. While the characters are fictional, the story is based on actual events. What would become of Jacob Miller? Would he ever get his life back again, or was a life behind bars all he would ever know? How had such a good, compassionate kid come to an act like this? What had gone so wrong in his life to have robbed him of his morals and allowed him to make such a dreadful choice?

CHILDREN'S BOOKS BY THE AUTHOR

After the Snowflakes *is a fully illustrated children's book about winter time activities. Each beautifully illustrated page shows a different event that celebrates fun things we can do after the snowflakes fall, including a few pages showing how different snowflakes could look. It ends with a playful poem about the uniqueness of snowflakes, encouraging the reader to get outside and enjoy the winter.*

✫✫✫✫✫✫✫

Sunny Boy *is an illustrated children's book that discusses the role of the sun from an animated perpective. He starts to feel rejected when people don't appreciate him, but comes to realize the importance of the role he plays in the world around him. It is also a story of relationships and working together, as he forms a true friendship with Whispi the Cloud.*

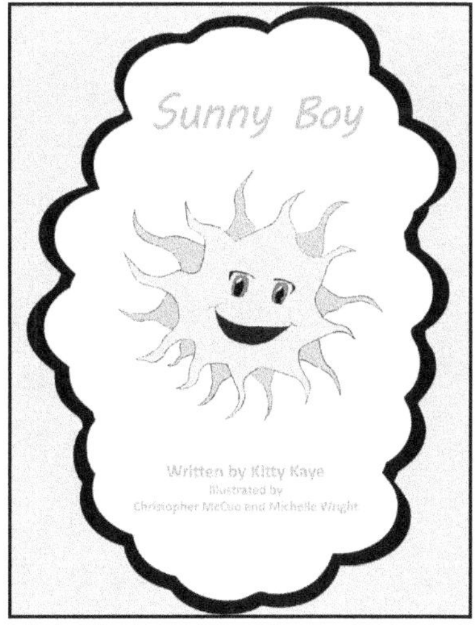

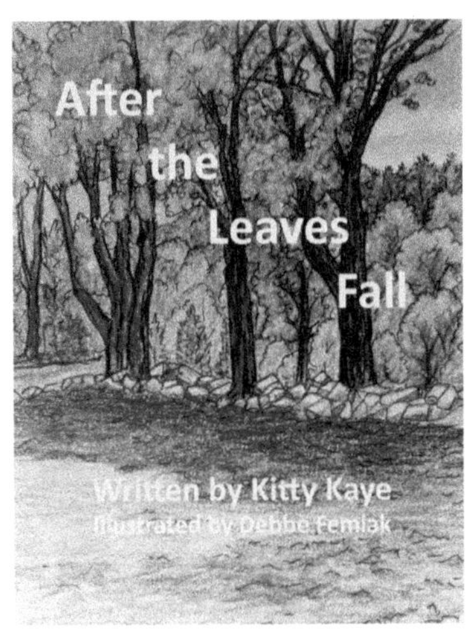

After the Leaves Fall is a beautifully illustrated children's book about the season of autumn. Each illustrated pages shows various activites to participate in after the leaves have fallen. Also included are pages showing the different shapes and colors of leaves. It winds down with a poem about autumn leaves, which encourages the reader to enjoy the colorful season of fall.

✯ ✯ ✯ ✯ ✯ ✯ ✯

Grandma Kitty's Coloring Book of Poetry is a book for coloring, filled with encouraging poetry verses. The children's verses are to help build self-esteem and promote acceptable behaviors. The adult verses are for those who have faced challenging situations. Each page has an illustration to color and is suitable for framing upon completion.

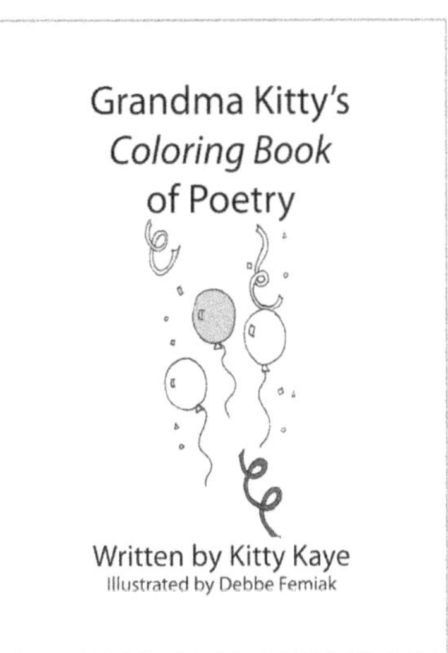